AMERICAN ★ HISTORY

NATIVE AMERICANS in Early North America

By Barbara M. Linde

Portions of this book originally appeared in
Early Native North Americans by Don Nardo.

LUCENT PRESS

Published in 2017 by
Lucent Press, an Imprint of Greenhaven Publishing, LLC
353 3rd Avenue
Suite 255
New York, NY 10010

Designer: Deanna Paternostro
Editor: Katie Kawa

Cataloging-in-Publication Data

Names: Linde, Barbara M.
Title: Native Americans in early North America / Barbara M. Linde .
Description: New York : Lucent Press, 2017. | Series: American history | Includes index.
Identifiers: ISBN 9781534560376 (library bound) | ISBN 9781534560383 (ebook)
Subjects: LCSH: Indians of North America--History--Juvenile literature.
Classification: LCC E77.4 L56 2017 | DDC 970.004'97--dc23

Printed in the United States of America

CPSIA compliance information: Batch #CW17KL: For further information contact Greenhaven Publishing LLC, New York, New York at 1-844-317-7404.

Please visit our website, www.greenhavenpublishing.com. For a free color catalog of all our high-quality books, call toll free 1-844-317-7404 or fax 1-844-317-7405.

Contents

Foreword	**4**
Setting the Scene: A Timeline	**6**
Introduction: A Rich and Complex History	**8**
Chapter One: Origin Theories	**12**
Chapter Two: The Earliest North Americans	**22**
Chapter Three: Native Americans of the West	**32**
Chapter Four: Native Americans of the Great Plains	**44**
Chapter Five: Early Native Americans of the Southeast	**54**
Chapter Six: Native Americans of the Northeastern Woodlands	**65**
Chapter Seven: Games, Weapons, and Intertribal Warfare	**76**
Epilogue: The European Onslaught	**86**
Notes	**93**
For More Information	**96**
Index	**98**
Picture Credits	**103**
About the Author	**104**

Foreword

The United States is a relatively young country. It has existed as its own nation for more than 200 years, but compared to nations such as China that have existed since ancient times, it is still in its infancy. However, the United States has grown and accomplished much since its birth in 1776. What started as a loose confederation of former British colonies has grown into a major world power whose influence is felt around the globe.

How did the United States manage to develop into a global superpower in such a short time? The answer lies in a close study of its unique history. The story of America is unlike any other—filled with colorful characters, a variety of exciting settings, and events too incredible to be anything other than true.

Too often, the experience of history is lost among the basic facts: names, dates, places, laws, treaties, and battles. These fill countless textbooks, but they are rarely compelling on their own. Far more interesting are the stories that surround those

basic facts. It is in discovering those stories that students are able to see history as a subject filled with life—and a subject that says as much about the present as it does about the past.

The titles in this series allow readers to immerse themselves in the action at pivotal historical moments. They also encourage readers to discuss complex issues in American history—many of which still affect Americans today. These include racism, states' rights, civil liberties, and many other topics that are in the news today but have their roots in the earliest days of America. As such, readers are encouraged to think critically about history and current events.

Each title is filled with excellent tools for research and analysis. Fully cited quotations from historical figures, letters, speeches, and documents provide students with firsthand accounts of major events. Primary sources bring authority to the text, as well. Sidebars highlight these quotes and primary sources, as well as interesting figures and events. Annotated bibliographies allow students to locate and evaluate sources for further information on the subject.

A deep understanding of America's past is necessary to understand its present and its future. Sometimes you have to look back to see how to best move forward, and that's certainly true when writing the next chapter in the American story.

Setting the Scene:

c.a. 1000 BC
The mound-building Adena people begin to thrive in the Ohio River valley.

c.a. AD 200
The giant Pyramid of the Sun is completed in the Native American city of Teotihuacan in Central America.

c.a. 1000 BC | **c.a. 300 BC** | **c.a. AD 200** | **c.a. 500–700** | **c.a. 850**

c.a. 300 BC
The mound-building Hopewell people begin spreading their influence through what is now the eastern United States.

c.a. 500-700
Use of the bow and arrow becomes widespread across North America.

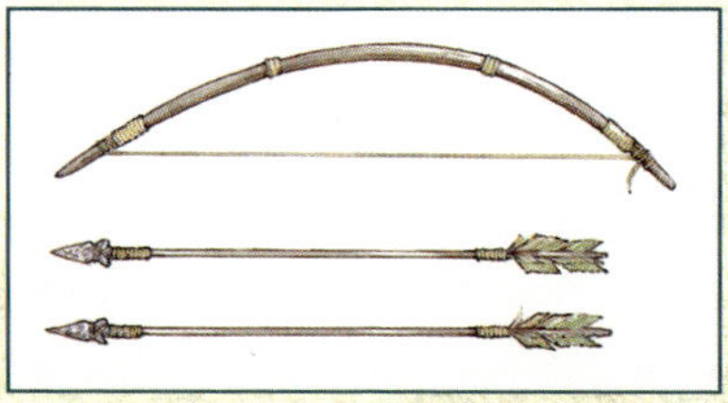

c.a 850
Native American groups living in the Great Plains begin practicing agriculture.

A Timeline

c.a. 1100–1300
The cultural golden age of the Ancestral Puebloans in the American Southwest.

c.a.1640
The Native American groups inhabiting the Great Plains begin using horses.

c.a. 1100–1300 | 1492 | c.a. 1570 | c.a.1640 | 1890

1492
Italian mariner Christopher Columbus lands in the Caribbean, a region then called the "Indies," and coins the term "Indians."

1890
The massacre at Wounded Knee in South Dakota marks the close of a long period of bloody fighting between Native Americans and whites.

c.a. 1570
The Iroquois Confederacy, an alliance of Native American groups in what is now New York State, is founded.

Introduction

A RICH AND COMPLEX HISTORY

Native Americans are descended from people who journeyed from Asia to North America across a land bridge thousands of years ago. When exactly did they arrive? Groups of scientists and historians differ when it comes to answering that question. Some believe evidence points to a migration that began 23,000 years ago, while others believe the first of these people did not reach North America until 15,000 years ago or even sooner. More DNA research is needed to provide them with a clear answer.

Although the date of their arrival in North America is still unknown, much more is understood about what happened to these people once they arrived in the Western Hemisphere. Over time, they spread out across both North America and South America, settling in groups that adapted to their natural surroundings. These groups were all unique, with their own foods, customs, religions, and social orders. Some lived as hunter-gatherers, but others eventually moved away from that nomadic lifestyle and began growing crops.

Life changed for Native Americans, who are also known as American Indians, when European settlers first arrived in the Western Hemisphere. These new settlers brought guns and other advanced weapons with them, which were used to help defeat the Native Americans and conquer their lands. In addition, Europeans brought diseases that Native Americans had no cure for or immunity to, such as smallpox, which wiped out huge portions of their population.

With their lands taken over and their numbers greatly reduced, the rich history of Native Americans was ignored for a long time. Over time, however, that mindset changed. Today, we know that the history of Native Americans in North America is rich and complex, and it is an important part of American history. As archaeologists continue to dig up artifacts left behind by Native Americans, it becomes easier to find the answers to questions about how they lived their lives before and after they first came into contact with Europeans. As such, an important part of American history has been preserved for future generations.

The past was filled with loss for Native Americans, and the present is filled with new struggles, but also a deep sense of cultural pride. However, the future looks even brighter because of the promise of deeper understanding.

Different Opinions on Archaeology

Although archaeological finds are helping people better understand and respect Native American history and culture, the work of unearthing the secrets of the ancient Native Americans is sometimes hampered by what is best described as a "culture gap" between archaeologists and Native Americans. Some groups have their own archaeologists. The Zunis and Hopis in the southwestern United States, for example, conduct digs and studies related to their own histories, and the Mashantucket Pequots in Connecticut have operated an extensive archaeological program on their reservation since 1983. Among other discoveries, they found the remains of a fort that was in use around 1675. Thousands of artifacts unearthed by the excavators can be seen in the tribe's museum, which opened in 1998.

These tribal excavations are the exception rather than the rule, though. Most archaeologists who dig up the remains of past Native American cultures are not Native Americans. As such, many Native Americans view their excavations with some degree of suspicion and discomfort. This stems mainly from a difference in the way Native Americans and non-Native Americans view digging up the graves and handling the remains of buried ancestors. Most white archaeologists believe that such excavations are justified because they advance human knowledge. In contrast, many Native Americans see tampering with burial sites as a serious spiritual violation. "The field of archaeology is a discipline that has been little understood in the Native American community," Zuni scholar Edmund J. Ladd pointed out. Ladd continued,

> *Digging about in the ancient tombs and robbing graves are activities Native Americans associate with witchcraft and consider to be fraught with the danger of [spiritual] contamination and death. Traditionally, most Indian people would not consider digging up another human being's remains.*[1]

Native American scholars such as Ladd believe that another aspect of the culture gap between Indian traditionalists and modern archaeologists is the way Native Americans have long viewed their own past. Descendants of the early European settlers have tended to have a strong fascination for what their own distant ancestors did. Many American Indians, by contrast, have been more oriented toward their present and future and fairly uninterested in their dim past. "Why dwell on the past?" one Native American elder said. "We have already been there ... and we can't do anything to change it."[2]

The Case of the Kennewick Man

During most of the 20th century, numerous American Indian communities regretted the excavation of ancient burials so much that they lobbied Congress to protect the gravesites. This effort reached its highest point in the 1990 Native American Graves Protection and Repatriation Act (NAGPRA). This law requires that all American Indian remains and cultural objects found on tribal or federal lands be turned over to the appropriate tribal authorities. The officials will then rebury these artifacts, which cannot be dug up later. Also, certain kinds of American Indian remains housed in museums and private collections can be reclaimed and buried by tribal authorities.

The effects of NAGPRA on North American archaeology may turn out to be significant. Hundreds of thousands of fragments of American Indian remains presently exist in public and private collections. Archaeologists worry, scholar Brian M. Fagan says,

> *that much of their scientific database for studying such topics as ancient diseases and diet will be lost forever with systematic reburial of ancient populations. They argue that reburial would deprive future generations of vital scientific information. Others, including many archaeologists, believe that reburial [is an] ethical issue and should outweigh any scientific gain.*[3]

Legal clashes have already occurred between supporters of NAGPRA and archaeologists who feel restricted by it. Perhaps the best-known case is that of Kennewick Man. This is the name given to an ancient set of human remains found in the Columbia River in Washington State in 1996. Anthropologist James Chatters and other experts examined the remains. They think that Kennewick Man is around 9,000 years old. Debates raged for many years about the origins of Kennewick Man. Some experts believed the remains were different enough from those of Native Americans to point to Kennewick Man belonging to a different racial group. If Kennewick Man was not an ancestor of Native Americans, some archaeologists argued, his remains could not be buried using NAGPRA as the reasoning behind the burial.

However, in 2015, a study showed that Kennewick Man's DNA was more closely linked to Native Americans than to any other group. As such, the Native Americans who had been fighting for the right to bury his remains got their wish. In 2016, it was confirmed that Kennewick Man could be given a Native American burial.

An archaeologist's work is often very painstaking and time-consuming.

The debate around the origins of Kennewick Man ended up being only one of many challenges to learning about North America's distant past. However, Fagan, among others, is optimistic that the disagreements that led to the creation of NAGPRA will give way "to a new era in which both groups cooperate, [although] somewhat cautiously." If a spirit of trust can be achieved, he has said, "the results can be rewarding." Indeed, discovering the details of when and how American Indians populated the continent can only be accomplished conclusively through archaeological excavation, and "the future of North American archaeology," Fagan points out, "lies in collaborative research, in which Native Americans play a leading role."[4]

Chapter One

ORIGIN THEORIES

In 1492, Christopher Columbus landed on a Caribbean island that the natives called *Guanahani*. He had not, as he had intended, reached the Indies (a word that—at the time—referred to part of Asia). Instead, he had arrived at an island that was part of the American continent.

Columbus recorded his first impression of the people in his log:

> *They ... brought us parrots and balls of cotton and spears and many other things, which they exchanged for the glass beads and hawks' bells. They willingly traded everything they owned.... They were well-built, with good bodies and handsome features.... They do not bear arms, and do not know them, for I showed them a sword, they took it by the edge and cut themselves out of ignorance. They have no iron. Their spears are made of cane.*[5]

There is now some disagreement about how these native peoples were named. The traditional story is that, since he believed he was in the Indies, Columbus called the native peoples he met Indians. A newer theory proposes that Columbus called the people either *gente en Dios* ("people of God"), or *los niños de la Endeo* ("children of God"); these names were later shortened to *Indios/Indian*. While the term Indian is still incorrect, it is often used, although the terms Native American and American Indian are considered to be more acceptable.

Although Columbus's explorations were limited to the Caribbean Islands, other early European explorers reached the mainland of North America. By the mid-1500s, Ponce De Leon, Álvar Núñez Cabeza de Vaca, Francisco Vázquez de Coronado, and Hernando de Soto had all encountered native

Native Americans are shown here greeting Christopher Columbus and his crew.

peoples throughout the southern parts of the present-day United States.

European scholars, leaders, and others were curious about these people. Who were they, and how long had they been in this remote place? How had they arrived, and how extensive was their civilization? As more Europeans explored and eventually settled in the New World, their curiosity continued. Over the years, several theories about the Indians were proposed and discussed. A few decades ago, researchers and scientists were sure they had found the definitive answer. Recently, however, new scientific discoveries have cast doubt on parts of that answer, and new ideas have come to the forefront.

Creation Myths

The first efforts to establish how the Native Americans had arrived in the Americas consisted of questioning the natives directly. Once communications had been established, European leaders and missionaries asked where they came from. The Native Americans had no formal histories, either written or oral, to help them answer such questions with certainty.

However, the natives did have religious traditions and creation myths that had been passed down orally over many generations. Based on these stories, many natives assumed their tribes had always been there, at least since their creator (often called the Great Spirit or Great Chief) had made them. Such creation tales varied between the groups and regions, but many held similarities to that of the Chelan people of what is now Washington State. Long ago, the story goes, the Great Chief fashioned the world:

> *Then he made the animals and the birds and gave them their names—Coyote, Grizzly Bear, Deer, Fox, Eagle, the four Wolf Brothers, Magpie, Bluejay, Hummingbird, and all the others. When he had finished his work, the creator called the animal people to him. "I am going to leave you," he said. "But I will come back. When I come again, I will make human beings. They will be in charge of you."*[6]

Many other Native American legends also describe a great migration that had occurred in the past. However, they were not clear about where that migration had begun. Some Native Americans in eastern North America claimed that their ancestors had come from the "land of the setting sun," or

This depiction of a creation story is displayed at The National Museum of the American Indian in Washington, D.C.

Columbus's Description of Native Americans

These words are part of Christopher Columbus's initial description of the people he called Indians, entered in his log in the fall of 1492:

As I saw that they were very friendly to us, and perceived that they could be much more easily converted to our holy faith by gentle means than by force, I presented them with some red caps, and strings of beads to wear upon the neck, and many other trifles of small value, wherewith they were much delighted, and became wonderfully attached to us. Afterwards they came swimming to the boats, bringing parrots, balls of cotton thread, javelins, and many other things which they exchanged for articles we gave them, such as glass beads, and hawk's bells … Weapons they have none, nor are acquainted with them, for I showed them swords which they grasped by the blades, and cut themselves through ignorance.[1]

1. Internet Medieval Sourcebook, "Christopher Columbus: Extracts from the Journal," Fordham University. www.fordham.edu/halsall/source/columbus1.html.

the West; while some western groups said the migrations began somewhere in the East.

European Explanations

The first European explorers who heard these stories viewed them as simplistic fables and dismissed them. Thereafter, European scholars searched for what they saw as more credible explanations for the origins of the Native Americans. Dozens of theories appeared in the 1500s and 1600s. Because the authors of these theories believed that the beginning of civilization happened in or near Europe and the regions around the Mediterranean Sea, they almost always envisioned migrations from that region.

For instance, one common thought was that the Native Americans were descended from Phoenicians or Carthaginians. The Phoenicians were skilled sailors from what is now Palestine who established extensive trade routes across the Mediterranean Sea between 1000 and 600 BC. One of their colonies, Carthage, in North Africa, eventually grew into a rich and mighty empire. Some 16th-century scholars believed that a number of Phoenician or Carthaginian sailors ventured too far out into the Atlantic Ocean and ended up in the Americas. Over time, their descendants had become the Native Americans. Other similar theories suggested that sailors from Egypt, Wales, or other regions of the Old World had gone off course and founded the New World populations.

All the scholars and writers who tried to explain the origins of the Native Americans were devout Christians. So it is not surprising that many of them turned to the Bible for inspiration. In 1567, for example, a Dutch theologian named Joannes Lumnius revisited the mystery of the lost tribes of Israel. According to the Bible, he pointed out, an Assyrian king had conquered the northern kingdom of Israel and carried away its people to what is now Iraq.[7] These Jews—members of 10 early Jewish groups—never returned to Palestine. What became of them? According to Lumnius, they somehow made their way across the Atlantic to the Americas, and their descendants became the Native Americans.

The Chelan Creation Myth

According to the Chelan Native American group of Washington State, the powerful supernatural being known as the Great Chief built the world and fashioned the major kinds of animals. Later, he instructed the Wolf Brothers to kill the beaver who lived in the water and divide his body into 12 pieces, which would become the first groups of human beings. The youngest of the wolf brothers succeeded in slaying the beaver. Then:

> *Youngest Brother gave other pieces to other animal people and told them where to go. They took the liver to Clearwater River, and it became the Nez Perce Indians. They took the heart across the mountains, and it became the Methow Indians. Other parts became the Spokane people, the Lake people, the Flathead people. Each of the eleven pieces became a different tribe. "There have to be twelve tribes," said Youngest Brother. "Maybe the Creator thinks that we should use the blood for the last one. Take the blood across the Shining Mountains and wake it up over there. It will become the Blackfeet. They will always look for blood."*[1]

1. Indigenous Peoples' Literature, "Chelan Creation Myth: Creation of the First Indians." www.indians.org/welker/firstind.htm.

Many Europeans accepted this idea and offered proof for it. One was a Portuguese traveler, Antonio Montezinos, who wrote, "It was a thrilling journey I took in South America. Now that I am back … I must share with you some incredible news. There is a Jewish Indian tribe living beyond the mountain passes of the Andes [Mountains]. Indeed, I myself … saw them observe the Jewish rituals."[8] The rituals that Montezinos claimed he witnessed were never verified, but for centuries to come, many Europeans continued to accept a Jewish ancestry for the Native Americans.

In fact, this notion survives today in Mormon beliefs. According to the Mormon scriptures (the Book of Mormon), the Jews who migrated to the Americas split into two groups—the Nephites and Lamanites. Because the Lamanites were evildoers, God cursed them and turned their skin dark. The Nephites, whose skin remained white, were eventually wiped out by the Lamanites, who became the Native Americans.

Another theory proposed by Europeans involved the legendary lost continent of Atlantis. Atlantis was supposedly a large mass of land that existed in the Atlantic Ocean before it sank beneath the waves in a huge catastrophe in ancient times. In 1535, a Spanish writer named Gonzalo Fernandez de Oviedo y Valdes proposed that the Atlanteans fled the island and then made their way to the nearby Americas, where they established the various Native American groups.

José de Acosta's Theory

It is interesting to note that today's most widely accepted explanation for the Native Americans' origins first appeared in the same period as the more fanciful ones. An inquisitive and hardworking Jesuit missionary, José de Acosta, traveled to the Americas in the mid-1500s and lived among the inhabitants for many years. After much careful thought, in 1590 he published his *Natural and Moral History of the Indies*. It contained a theory about the peopling of North America that no one else had considered—that the

HISTORIA
NATVRAL
Y
MORAL DELAS
INDIAS,
EN QVE SE TRATAN LAS COSAS notables del cielo, y elementos, metales, plantas, y animales dellas: y los ritos, y ceremonias, leyes, y gouierno, y guerras de los Indios.
Compuesta por el Padre Ioseph de Acosta Religioso de la Compañia de Iesus.
DIRIGIDA A LA SERENISSIMA Infanta Doña Isabella Clara Eugenia de Austria.

CON PRIVILEGIO.
Impresso en Seuilla en casa de Iuan de Leon.
Año de 1590.

Missionaries such as José de Acosta provided some of the first written descriptions of Native American culture and beliefs.

Native Americans had originated in eastern Asia.

Acosta saw that several of the same animal species existed on the continents of Asia and North America, and he concluded that the beasts of one continent must have migrated there from the other continent. This meant that the two landmasses must be connected at some spot. (At the time, most of North America and northeastern Asia had yet to be explored by Europeans, so the existence of such a connection seemed at least possible.) Furthermore, Acosta said, if animals could migrate from one landmass to the other, so could people. "We may easily infer from these arguments," he wrote,

> *that the first Indians went to inhabit the Indies [i.e., North America] more by land than by sea; or if there were any navigation, it was neither great nor difficult [since] the one world [continent] is continued and [joined] with the other, or at the least they approach nearer unto another in some parts.*[9]

Gradually, Acosta said, the Native Americans moved from Asia into North America and spread across the continent.

For a long time, Acosta's theory of the Native Americans' origins remained merely one of many that were proposed and debated in European scholarly circles. Few people accepted it, partly because it presupposed that the peoples of North America were very ancient. It was more fashionable in those days to suggest that the Indians were offshoots of European peoples, which required their arrival in the Americas to be a fairly recent event.

The Bering Land Bridge

Over time, however, more and more scientists suspected that the Native Americans were a much older people than had been previously thought. Prominent among them was archaeologist and anthropologist Samuel Haven of the American Antiquarian Society. In 1855 he published an important study titled *Archaeology of the United States*. Like Acosta, Haven looked toward Asia for the original homeland of the earliest Native Americans. "All their characteristic affinities [traits and habits]," Haven wrote, "are found in the early conditions of Asiatic races."[10] These words were written more than a century after Russian explorer Vitus Bering had discovered the strait named for him, lying between Alaska and Siberia. Because he had shown that no land bridge exists between them, most scholars found the idea of an ancient migration from Asia to North America hard to believe. They gave Haven's proposal about the Native Americans a cool reception.

Yet Acosta and Haven were eventually proved right. By the 1960s, enough geological evidence had been found to verify that 18,000 years ago (16,000 BC) sea levels were some 300 feet (91 m) lower

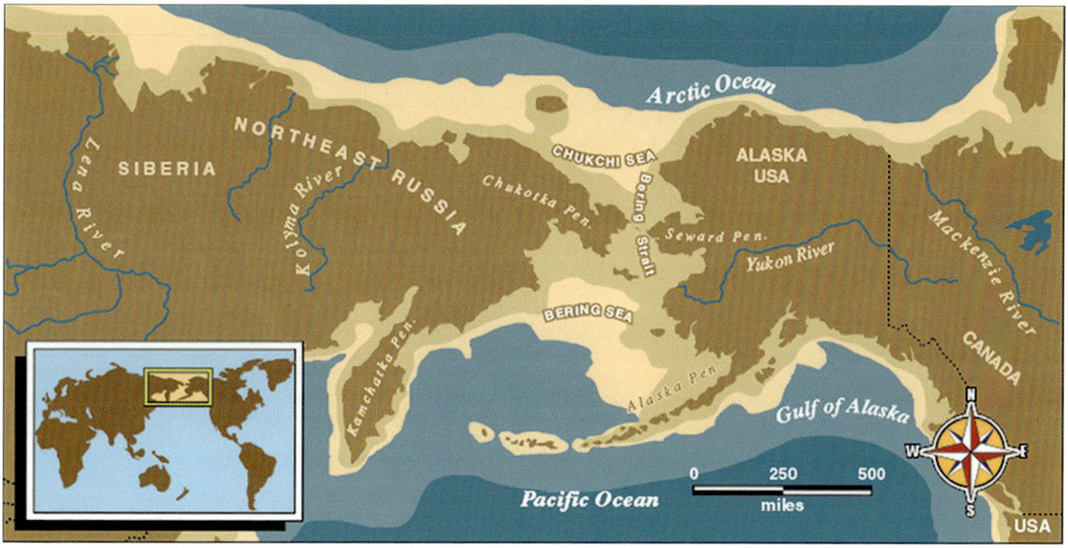

This map shows the Bering Land Bridge and the route animals and humans took to cross from Siberia to Alaska and beyond.

than they are today. Where the Bering Strait now exists, there was a stretch of exposed continental shelf thousands of square miles in extent—now called both the Bering Land Bridge and Beringia. The most recent evidence suggests that Beringia first appeared about 75,000 years ago, during the last major ice age. It shrank considerably during a warming trend lasting from about 40,000 to 25,000 years ago. However, then it expanded once more and remained in place until roughly 11,000 years ago.

In the period lasting from about 18,000 to 12,000 years ago, Beringia was largely a subarctic wilderness with few trees. However, it had enough small plants, grasses, and freshwater rivers and ponds to sustain small populations of large animals. Among the beasts that evidence now confirms traveled from eastern Siberia, across the land bridge, and into what are now Alaska and Canada were woolly mammoths, which were huge, elephant-like creatures. Other imposing animals that dwelled in Beringia included ground sloths 9.8 feet (3 m) long, beavers the size of black bears, bison with horns about 6 feet (2 m) long, along with camels, reindeer, horses, bears, mountain lions, and wolves.

Gradual Migration

Thus, the very conditions that Acosta long ago envisioned—an expanse of land bridging Asia and North America and migrations of large animals across that expanse—did in fact exist at one time. His assumption that early humans crossed the land bridge, too, was at last a compelling idea that could not be ignored. The exact date of the migration is uncertain. However, a good deal of evidence indicates that it did occur. Also, it appears to have taken place within a certain general time frame—between 15,000 and 11,000 years ago.

First, the remains of sites occupied by ancient hunter-gatherers have been found both in eastern Siberia and Alaska. One of the main Siberian sites is a cave at Dyuktai in the Aldan River Valley. Like other Siberian sites, it contains not only bones from butchered animals, but also stone tools characteristic of these hunters—small, sharpened stone blades used as spear points and knives. Archaeologists refer to them as microblades. Nearly identical kinds of microblades have been found in ancient sites in the Tanana Valley, 60 miles (97 km) southeast of Fairbanks, Alaska, and at other Alaskan sites. Clearly, people from the same Stone Age culture occupied all these sites.

The dating of these sites is also striking because it sets up a believable scenario for the hunters' eastward migration. The Dyuktai Cave site dates from about 18,000 years ago. The Alaskan sites range in age from about 13,700 to 11,000 years ago. This suggests that some of the bands of Asian hunters reached Beringia by 15,000 years ago and that some of their descendants began moving into Alaska about a millennium later.

It is clear that only some of the hunters migrated from region to region; probably small groups followed moving animal herds further eastward or southeastward, while most members of their communities stayed put and lived out their lives. Thus, as scholar Philip Kopper pointed out, these periodic treks into new hunting grounds were not part of some overriding plan but, rather, random and gradual events. "There is no reason to believe that these people knew where they were going," he wrote,

> *or even that they knew they were going anywhere. Beringia should not be seen as just an avenue of transit, but as a place where people lived, some of whom moved on. The term "migration" mistakenly implies intentional relocation, when actually the pace might have been so slow that each generation of immigrants thought they were simply moving to the next overlook or game-rich valley.*[11]

This archaeological evidence is strongly supported by recent studies that compared the physical characteristics and DNA of Native Americans to certain Asian inhabitants of Siberia. These studies confirm that the two groups were at one time closely related. The DNA evidence also suggests that the Asian migrants did not all arrive in Alaska at once. Rather, they came in waves over the course of 2,000 to 4,000 years.

These primitive hunter-gatherers,

A New Theory of Migration

A new study published in 2016 proposed a different idea of how the first humans came to North America. Researchers took sediment core samples from a glacial lake that they believe lies along the last part of the migration passage. Their testing of plant and animal DNA indicates that the area did not have enough plant or animal life before about 12,600 years ago to provide food for the migrating peoples. They believe that even though the passage was open, the first groups of people must have come from a different route. The researchers suggest that these first humans came from somewhere along the Pacific coast, possibly east by boat or somehow using sea ice. According to their research, later groups of people did use the passage—but not the very first group.

North America's earliest human immigrants, had no idea, of course, that they were making history. As Fagan wrote,

> *it was a watershed in human development, a moment to pause and wonder at humanity's startling ability to adapt to the extremes of life on planet Earth. Human beings first evolved in the relatively undemanding tropical environments of Africa, then progressively mastered ever more harsh climates … Eventually they came to the frontiers of a vast continent. Soon they were to wander into the heart of the Americas and explode into a new chapter of human history.*[12]

Chapter Two

THE EARLIEST NORTH AMERICANS

Even though other theories are coming out, most scholars still adhere to the idea that the first settlers came from eastern Asia, across Beringia. However, they are still not certain how these migrants settled North America. Archaeologists and other researchers have developed a theory that is based on tools, weapons, animal bones, and other evidence, which has been collected from sites in Canada and around the United States.

Researchers and other experts use the term Paleo-Indians to describe these early inhabitants. The term *Paleo*, or *Palaeo*, is from the Greek word for "ancient" or "prehistoric". Most experts believe that the Paleo-Indians were the first permanent settlers in North America and that they began to arrive about 15,000 years ago.

Scholars have given the name Clovis peoples to one early group of Paleo-Indians, because the stone tools that provide the first evidence of their culture were found near Clovis, New Mexico. These spear points were made from jasper, obsidian, and other stones. The Clovis peoples were hunter-gatherers who quickly spread all over the continent, as shown by discoveries of Clovis points in over 1,500 sites around North America. The oldest dated point, from Texas, is about 13,500 years old. This find shows that in about 1,000 years, bands of Clovis hunters spread from Northern Canada to Texas, about 2,500 miles (4,023 km).

Researchers also discovered that the Clovis points were not found among artifacts from Siberia. They conclude that the Clovis point was first made in North America.

Some researchers have uncovered bones and other artifacts that indicate a culture that predates the Clovis peoples, but there is not yet enough data to draw firm conclusions.

The Folsom peoples followed the Clovis peoples, and there is some evidence that the two cultures may have overlapped for a few hundred years. These people used a shorter stone point than the Clovis peoples did. Their name comes from the discovery of the first stone points near Folsom, New Mexico. Unlike the spreading Clovis groups, the Folsom peoples stayed primarily in the Great Plains and Texas.

The Paleo-Indian era ended about 11,000 years ago, around 7,000 BC. The groups following them are called Archaic cultures. These peoples flourished until about 500 BC. The Archaic groups tended to stay in one area, instead of migrating. They learned to adapt to their environment, which helped to create distinct cultures, traditions, and languages.

The Clovis Peoples

The speed at which the Clovis peoples populated North America is perhaps not so surprising when one considers that they were primarily roving hunters. Studies of early modern peoples who hunted elephants and other large game were conducted in Africa and other parts of the world in the 1800s and 1900s. These studies revealed that the hunters most often followed the herds, which sometimes ranged over hundreds of square miles. The Clovis hunters must have done the same. Their chief prey seems to have been mammoths, huge animals that likely migrated up to 200 miles (322 km) in a given season. Therefore, a single band of hunters following such a herd would have become familiar with a very large amount of territory.

To bring down mammoths, giant sloths, moose, reindeer, and other large prey, these hunters used weapons tipped with their signature stone point. The average Clovis point is about four to six inches (10 to 15 cm) long. It is also sharpened on both sides. A typical Clovis point is fluted; it has a recessed channel carved into the stone near the bottom of the point. Most experts think that a hunter laid a narrow, rounded wooden shaft into it and tied the shaft and point together securely. Probably the hunter carried several such small, lightweight, pointed shafts while stalking game. They would need only one heavier spear with a groove carved in the top. The hunter could push one of the pointed shafts into the groove and then jab the weapon into the prey. Afterward, the broken or dulled point could be removed from the animal and a new pointed shaft could be slipped onto the end of the spear in preparation for the next hunt.

The Clovis hunters likely used such spears at close range, to stab and finish off large animals that were already wounded or otherwise incapacitated, possibly drinking at a watering hole. For initial, long-range strikes, they placed their premade pointed shafts into a more ingenious weapon called an atlatl. (The term *atlatl* is the name given to the weapon by the Aztec Indians of central and southern Mexico. Stone Age hunters in what is now the United States and other parts of the world had a wide range of names for it, but modern scholars came to use the

Aztec term for all of them.)

About 18 inches (46 cm) long, the atlatl was a throwing stick composed of a wooden handle attached to a wooden socket or groove. The hunter inserted the rear end of a premade pointed shaft into the groove and used a forceful overhand motion to send the sharpened point flying through the air. The atlatl produced considerably more forward momentum than was possible to achieve with the arm alone. This meant it could fire a point farther than the hunter could throw an ordinary spear and the point struck the prey with more force. The atlatl could be used one-handed, either on land or from a boat. Scholars think that Clovis hunters may have hunted whales and other sea animals along the coast.

The damage these weapons could inflict has been revealed by the recently discovered remains of mammoths and other large beasts. The bones of a mammoth slain by Clovis hunters were found in Murray Springs, Arizona. Another mammoth, the remains of which were discovered at Naco, Arizona, died with eight Clovis points imbedded in its body. It is unknown whether eight hunters each struck the beast once, four hunters each hit it twice, or some other combination. Noted archaeologist George Frison suggested that groups of hunters worked in unison to hunt such a large animal. One hunter likely distracted the mammoth, he said, after which two or more hunters unleashed their atlatls. It became vital to develop such teamwork, Frison and other scholars pointed out, because a beast of this size was of tremendous value to the community. A single mammoth, Brian Fagan pointed out,

> *could provide meat for weeks on end, and, if dried, for much of the winter,*

In 2012, a fifth-grade boy found a Clovis point on a beach in New Jersey. Archaeologists think the buried blade might have come to the surface during beach restoration efforts after Hurricane Sandy. The 14,000-year-old blade is now part of the Smithsonian collection, and the finder has a casting of it.

The Solutrean Theory

Although most scholars accept the theory that Siberian hunter-gatherers crossed into Alaska about 14,000 years ago, some suggest that in addition a second group of Stone Age people might have entered North America from the East. The so-called Solutrean hypothesis was proposed in 1998 by scholars Dennis Stanford and Bruce Bradley. By examining stone tools found along the Chesapeake Bay and other Mid-Atlantic sites, they contend that the Clovis hunters of the Americas might have borrowed the idea for their projectile points from the ancient European Solutrean culture, whose members fashioned somewhat similar points some 20,000 years ago. They are the only two cultures to use this type of point. It is possible, Stanford and Bradley say, that bands of Solutrean hunters crossed broad patches of pack ice in the North Atlantic and made it into what is now Canada, and then traveled down the Atlantic coast. Critics of the hypothesis say that such an ocean crossing would have been too difficult. However, they cannot definitively rule it out.

too. Hides, tusks, bones, and pelts were used to make household possessions and weapons, for shelter, and for clothing. Precious fat from the internal organs could be melted down and used for cooking and burning in [crude oil] lamps. [13]

Sophisticated Clovis Lodges

Though big game kills were valuable to the community, the Clovis peoples likely also relied on other food sources. According to Fagan:

> *Undoubtedly they took not only big Ice Age species, but medium-sized animals like deer, and small rabbits and other mammals, as well. They must also have explored wild plant foods in spring, summer, and fall, as well perhaps as fish and other aquatic resources when the occasion arose. While the hunting of large mammals was sometimes important, and the people wandered far and wide in search of them, we can be sure that there were many distinctive adaptations to locally plentiful and predictable resources, which are not yet reflected in the archaeological record.* [14]

While researching the Clovis peoples, scholars have discovered how adaptable, resourceful, and clever its members were.

Researchers believe they were adept at using plants for both food and medicine. They probably made grinding tools to make effective use of the plants. To cook the plentiful Pleistocene turtles, the people made roasting pits.

In the last decades of the 20th century, evidence came to light showing that at least some of the Clovis peoples lived in sophisticated handmade lodges, not in caves. For example, excavations at an 11,000-year-old site in Virginia's Shenandoah Valley revealed the remains of a semipermanent Clovis camp. From a careful study of the soil, diggers determined that rows of wooden posts, by now rotted away, had long ago been driven vertically into the ground. These posts became the framework for a wattle lodge some 36 feet (11 m) long. (Wattle is an interwoven mix of twigs, branches, reeds, and other plant materials.) Up to thirty people had shelter from the elements in this dwelling, which took the excavators by surprise. "Paleo-Indians weren't supposed to put that much effort into a house,"[15] University of Delaware scholar Jay F. Custer remarked after inspecting the site.

The Folsom Peoples

The Folsom hunters followed the Clovis peoples in North America, but the Folsom peoples created a different style of weaponry. Folsom points are about two inches (5 cm) long, which is considerably shorter than Clovis points. Most Folsom points are also thinner than Clovis versions, with a symmetrical, leaflike structure. In addition, the fluted groove in a Folsom point generally runs nearly the entire length of the blade.

Almost all the Folsom sites that have been discovered contain the remains of

The differences between Folsom points and Clovis points is evident in this photograph.

Using an Atlatl

In the 1540s, a member of the expedition of Spaniard Hernando de Soto, the first European to see the Mississippi River, saw some Native Americans using an atlatl and later described it in writing:

> *One soldier was wounded with … a dart … [which] is thrown with a wooden strip [the atlatl] … Our Spaniards had never seen this weapon before that day in any part of Florida through which they had traveled … The strip is of wood two-thirds of a yard in length, and is capable of sending a dart with such great force that it has been seen to pass completely through a man armed with a coat of mail [armor made of metal scales sewn or glued to a heavy jerkin]. In Peru, the Spaniards feared this weapon more than any others the Indian possessed, for the arrows there were not so fierce as those of Florida.*[1]

1. Garcilaso De La Vega, *Florida of the Inca,* trans. John and Jeannette Varner. Houston, TX: University of Texas Press, 1951, p. 597.

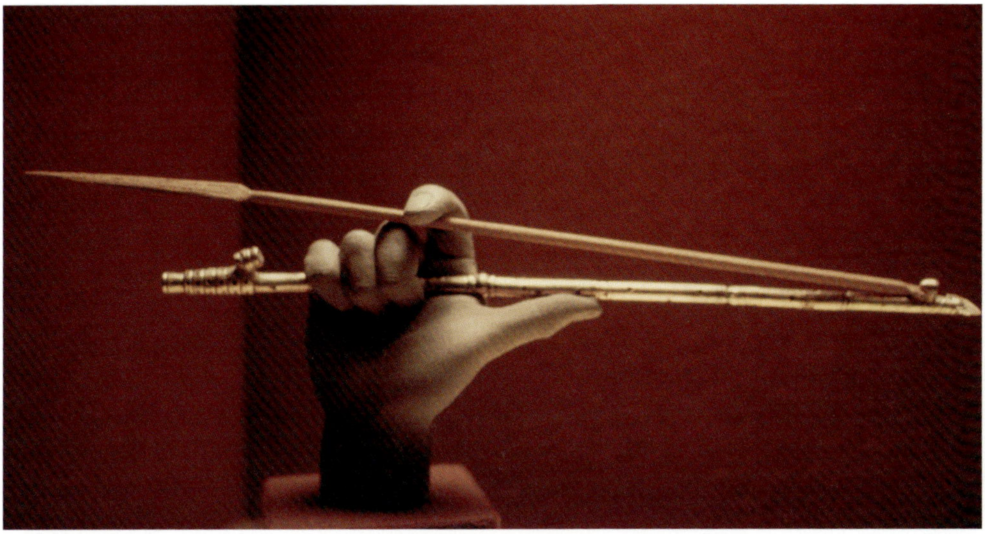

This image shows how an atlatl was used.

bison rather than mammoths. It appears that the physical differences between Folsom and Clovis points were at least in part related to differences in the prey themselves. Because bison are considerably smaller than mammoths, smaller stone points may have been sufficient to bring down bison. While Clovis points are found in many areas around the country, Folsom points have so far been discovered mostly in the central and western states. No other artifacts have been found yet, so researchers do not know much about the culture.

The transition from mammoth to bison hunting was not a matter of choice for the Paleo-Indians. Approximately 12,900 years ago, right at the close of the Clovis period, many of the large Ice Age mammals, including the mammoth and giant sloth, went extinct. At first, scholars were unable to explain how these so-called megafauna disappeared so abruptly. Then, in the 1960s, Professor Paul Martin of the University of Arizona proposed a new theory. The Stone Age hunters drove these beasts to extinction, he said, by killing large numbers of them in a relatively short span of time.

This overkill hypothesis seemed believable at first. However, over time, experts came to see it as only one of several factors that wiped out the megafauna. Other evidence has revealed a series of major fluctuations in climate; for example, the end of the Ice Age brought both

This hunting scene envisions what wildlife might have looked like very long ago.

rising temperatures and periodic serious droughts, which the larger animals were increasingly unable to cope with.

Still another possible factor came to light in 2007. University of Oregon archaeologists Douglas J. Kennett and Jon M. Erlandson announced they had found evidence that a natural disaster had ended the Clovis age. A small comet or large meteor struck the glaciers then covering the region just north of the Great Lakes, they said. The proof consists of a carbon-rich layer found at a certain level in the soil at more than 50 separate Clovis sites. "Highest concentrations of extraterrestrial impact materials occur in the Great Lakes area and spread out from there," Kennett stated,

> *It would have had major effects on humans [as well as the larger animals]. Immediate effects would have been in the North and East, producing shockwaves, heat, flooding, wildfires, and a reduction and fragmentation of the human population ... This was a massive continental scale, if not global, event.*[16]

This extraterrestrial impact theory has yet to be accepted by the majority of North American archaeologists. In 2010, researchers analyzing pollen from Folsom sites concluded that environmental changes, not extraterrestrial impact, ended the Clovis age. They believe that the Folsom peoples originated in the northern areas and gradually migrated south. The extraterrestrial hypothesis shows the opposite—that the Folsom people migrated from south to north. Research continues on these questions. Scientists hope that advanced methods, including radiocarbon dating, will soon provide more definitive conclusions.

The Archaic Period

Following the Folsom culture, there was another larger transition with more lasting results. Around 10,000 years ago, major climatic changes occurred that brought about the end of the Paleo-Indian phase and the opening of the long era of the Archaic Native Americans. University of Arizona scholar Arrell M. Gibson summarized the environmental changes that caused Native American cultures to become more specific to regions and different from each other:

> *The glacial ice cap retreated northward. The weather all over North America changed drastically as the climatic patterns we know today with regional variations began to emerge. Thus, the great integrating force of rather constant, continent-wide, mild climate, which had produced a homogeneous [more or less uniform] Paleo-Indian culture, faded. While the eastern portion of North America remained humid and well-watered, arid plains and deserts formed in the central and western sections. This evolving regional climatic variation produced ecological alterations. Swamps and bogs dried up. The coarse savanna grasses which had sustained*

Domesticated Plants in Early Virginia Indian Society

As the Native Americans settled into areas and were less nomadic, plants and gardening became important to their culture and way of life:

Virginia Indians began domesticating plants to be used as a food source following the Ice Age. As the climate warmed, their lives became less nomadic and the conditions improved for husbanding certain plants—sunflower, knotweed, and little barley at first, and then the so-called three sisters of maize, beans, and squash …

During the Paleo-Indian Period (16,000–8500 BC) and into the beginning of the Archaic Period (8500–1000 BC), Virginia Indians hunted and gathered in the large forests that dominated the landscape. Gradually their lifestyles became more sedentary, and they began to cultivate domesticated plants as a food source. As the climate warmed and rivers created flood plains with nutrient-rich soil, they encouraged wild plants by weeding and replanting seeds. Trash piles also improved the soil, and Indians found them to be ideal spots for gardens. Although there has been some disagreement over the years, scholars largely agree that eastern North America is one of just ten sites worldwide where plants were independently domesticated. (Those who demur argue that domesticated species dispersed northward from Mexico.) The first domesticates included sunflower, cucurbit gourd, knotweed, sumpweed, chenopod, little barley, and maygrass, and together are known as the Eastern Agricultural Complex. Ironically, the cultivated forms of these species are now mostly extinct, with some still surviving in the wild.[1]

1. Quoted in *Encyclopedia Virginia* staff, "Domesticated Plants in Early Virginia Indian Society," *Encyclopedia Virginia*. www.encyclopediavirginia.org/Domesticated_Plants_in_Early_Virginia_Indian_Society_Uses_of.

the mammoth … were replaced by shorter grasses that favored the smaller bison, antelope, deer, elk, and other species familiar today.[17]

Archaic Native Americans became highly skilled at hunting these and other small animals, as well as catching fish in lakes and ocean inlets. Evidence suggests that most of these peoples supplemented

Maize, shown here, became a vital crop for many Native American groups.

their meat supplies by foraging for plants more so than the Paleo-Indians had. It was possibly the increased knowledge of and experimentation with plants that led to the discovery of agriculture in the Archaic period. Not all Indian groups became farmers. Of those who did, some came to rely on their crops more than others. Also, agriculture was often a supplement to hunting and gathering, which remained important sources of food.

The exact manner in which agriculture developed in the Americas and the dates in which farming appeared in various regions is unknown. New research suggests that Archaic peoples from southern Arizona developed agricultural skills. When they migrated to the Mesa Verde/Colorado Plateau region, they introduced these skills to that group of archaic peoples. Cultivation of maize (a kind of corn), squash, beans, and pumpkins had become commonplace in what is now Mexico by 9,500 years ago; the American southwest by 7,500 years ago; and the eastern United States by 3,000 years ago.

Population increase and additional migrations during the Archaic period resulted in the formation of many regional groups and tribes, each of which adopted the food-producing customs, housing, and use of tools and utensils that best fit local conditions. Diversification occurred in spoken languages as well. By the eve of contact with white Europeans, more than 300 distinct languages were spoken in North America. Since the Native Americans groups are so different, the most effective way to examine their cultures is by region.

Chapter Three

NATIVE AMERICANS OF THE WEST

The western United States includes the subregions of the Northwest Coast, the Far West, and the Southwest. Each subregion breaks down into smaller, more localized regions. For example, the Northwest Coast extends from northern California to southern Alaska. The Far West consists of the Great Basin of Utah and Nevada, California, and the high plateau of inland Oregon, Washington, and Idaho. Arizona, New Mexico, and parts of nearby states make up the Southwest.

The Western Region

From the late Archaic times onward, most Native American groups stayed in one subregion, with long-term settlements replacing the earlier migratory way of life. However, a small group of hunter-gatherers would often travel a relatively short distance to hunt or collect food, and bring it back to the larger group's settlement.

One exception to the generally more permanent lifestyle of the Native Americans in the West was the Apache. Originally living in northwestern Canada and eastern Alaska, these peoples gradually migrated through the Great Plains and foothills of the Rocky Mountains to the modern-day southwestern United States and northwestern deserts of Mexico. Many scholars believe this migration took place between 1450 and the early 1500s. One theory about the origin of the name Apache is that the Zuni and Tewa tribes who were already living in the Southwest called these newcomers *Apachu*, their word for stranger or enemy. Their own name for themselves was *Nde*, meaning "the people".

Over time, these groups became experts at adapting to the local terrain, climate, natural supplies, and food sources. Because the regions themselves were so varied, the lifestyles also

This image shows Apaches in war dress.

became quite different from one another. Languages, customs, building techniques, and arts and craftwork all took on uniquely distinctive patterns. Still the various groups seemed to have a robust and extensive trade of goods as well as cultural practices.

The Native American tribes of the West include the Haida, the Tlingit, the Ute, the Pomo, and the Hopi. These peoples all exhibited the rich diversity among the various Native American cultures.

The Pacific Northwest Coast

The Pacific Northwest Coast region consists of a strip of well-forested territory between 100 and 200 miles (160 and 320 km) wide bordering the Pacific Ocean. It stretches from Yukutat Bay in the Gulf of Alaska to Cape Mendocino in northern California. The Queen Charlotte Islands, Vancouver Island, and other offshore islands are part of the region. The Coast Ranges and Cascade Mountains form the eastern boundary. Summers there tended to be cool, while winters were mild and wet. The plentiful rainfall in most years made the forests in the area dense and lush, producing large numbers of plants to eat or build with. These same woodlands were crawling with animal species—deer, elk, bears, raccoons, rabbits, and many others—to hunt. At the same time, the nearby sea contained whales, seals, salmon, trout, shellfish, and other creatures that the groups hunted or trapped. "There are few places in the world," the late American archaeologist Gordon Willey remarked, "where land and sea combine to offer such a rich and regular bounty for human consumption, and the Indians of the Northwest Coast … exploited it to the full."[18]

About 30 groups, including the Chinook, Makah, Nootka, Salish, Tillamook, and Tlingit, comprised the peoples of this region. Much is known about their lives and habits, in part because of a fortunate discovery made in 1969. It consisted of the remains of an entire Makah town located at Ozette on Washington's Olympic Peninsula. About 500 years ago, a devastating

Totem Poles

The Tlingit, Haida, Bella Coola, Chinook, Tsimshian, and Coast Salish peoples of the Pacific Northwest made totem poles. They were usually between 9 and 60 feet (3 and 18 m) high, and made of western red cedar. A master carver, generally a male, and his helpers worked on the sculptures for between three and nine months. The poles consisted of carved figures of ancestors, the family crest, animals, and supernatural beings. Every figure and color used had a special meaning, and the carvings were arranged to tell a story.

These early peoples did not have written languages, so the totem poles were an important means of communication. Heraldic poles placed in front of the house gave information about the family. Memorial poles honored an important dead person. Mortuary poles often contained the remains of the deceased, placed in small boxes near the top of the pole. A person might commission a potlatch pole to symbolize the bounty of his potlatch ceremony. House frontal poles stood in front of a house, and sometimes had an opening near the bottom that provided an entrance to the house. Totem poles located near the water specified the fishing and other boundaries for the group or village.

Totem poles were intricately carved and beautifully decorated.

Peoples of the Northwest Coast, such as the Makah shown here, relied heavily on the sea.

mudslide buried 6 longhouses, preserving much of their contents. So far, more than 50,000 artifacts have been found on the site, including baskets, fishing nets, weapons, and dishes. Current members of the Makah group have created a museum and research center at the dig site.

These and finds made at other Northwest Coast sites show, among other things, how the ancient inhabitants obtained their food. Agriculture was not widespread in the area because of the abundance of animals that were hunted on land and in the sea, and wild plants that were foraged. The men used wooden slats to build rectangular fishing traps, which they submerged in the water. They caught fish in nets and cleverly embedded rows of sharpened sticks in streams to impale migrating salmon. Hunters paddled cedar canoes out into the ocean and hurled razor-sharp harpoons to kill whales, sea otters, and seals. People burned certain oily fish like candles to provide light after the sun went down; these later came to be called candlefish. Meanwhile, women gathered basketfuls of strawberries, blueberries, elderberries, as well as the roots of the camas, wapato, and bracken fern. Many researchers believe that the abundance of food contributed to the development of the tiered society.

The houses at Ozette and many other northwestern sites stood in well-organized rows, usually facing the beach. They were made of huge logs stacked horizontally and notched at the ends to fit snugly together. The inside walls were faced with cedar planks. Multifamily dwellings each

Excavations of the Ozette village confirm the Makah story about a great slide. The excavation and artifacts are now part of the Makah Cultural and Research Center in Neah Bay, Washington.

had a spacious central room with one or more stone hearths (used for fireplaces) shared by all, along with wooden platforms that rose in tiers around it. Separated from one another by wooden screens or woven mats, these upper areas were for sleeping.

The structure of the houses at Ozette also reflected the residents' stratified social system. The highest-ranking member of a household slept on the highest platform, for instance, and clan heads and family members of chiefs had more authority, rights, and privileges than commoners and slaves. Status was also defined by degree of wealth, including the amount of possessions one owned or land one controlled. High-ranking members, especially chiefs, flaunted their wealth and status through large-scale celebrations called potlatches. In a potlatch, which could last for days, the guests feasted while the host impressed them by distributing loads of valuable goods among them. His stature was measured "by the grandness of his hospitality," Kopper explained.

> *Not only did he provide vast amounts of food, but he tested his guests' worthiness by their ability to consume [in] a kind of competition. Huge ceremonial bowls—sometimes boats—were filled with delicacies such as salmon roe or berries preserved in fish oil. Then the guest's party would be challenged to eat it all or lose stature before the other guests and be humiliated by the host.*[19]

Groups of the Great Basin and High Plateaus

The Native Americans of the Great Basin lived in material simplicity when compared to the peoples of the Northwest. This is because the rugged mountains and plains of Nevada and Utah, between the Sierra Nevada and the Rocky Mountains, were arid and supported few forests and little large game. Therefore, the tribes of the Great Basin, which include the Ute, Goshute, Western Shoshone, Paiute, and Washoe, hunted mostly small game.

This scene envisions the daily life of Great Basin peoples of Nevada and Utah.

The highlight of this activity was the annual rabbit hunt, which the first whites in the area witnessed and recorded. Hunters from several families pieced together an enormous net made of plant fibers. A mix of men, women, and children then used sticks to beat the ground and sagebrush, which caused the rabbits to run toward the net. Afterward, there was a feast and a celebration.

Then the tribe split up into individual units of one or two families to make foraging for food easier. The families moved from place to place within the Great Basin collecting seasonal berries, nuts, seeds, cacti, and other plants. Their lack of material possessions made these migrations easier. These seasonal travels "were carefully orchestrated," one scholar writes. "They were nomads not only in the horizontal plane but also in the vertical, taking advantage of the mountains' various ecological zones. Piñon pine nuts collected in large quantities grew at about 5,000 to 6,000 feet."[20]

One exception to this strictly hunter-gatherer existence was the Fremont culture, named for the Fremont River Valley, where their sites were first discovered. They flourished in the high-altitude parts of the Great Basin from about 600 to 1300. The Fremont peoples grew maize to supplement their hunting and foraging. They lived in pit houses similar to those common in the Southwest, which has led some scholars to propose that they migrated from that region into the basin.

Meanwhile, in the high plateaus lying north of the Great Basin, groups such as the Yakama, Klamath, Cayuse, Columbia, and Nez Perce developed a very different lifestyle. These plateaus are heavily forested in some areas, so they hunted wild game, including deer, antelope, elk, beaver, rabbits, and numerous species of birds. Also, the

Distinctive Pomo Baskets

The Pomo people of northern California developed basket-making skills to the level of high art, and skills that developed millennia ago were passed down through the generations to modern times. The late archaeologist and anthropologist Alfred L. Kroeber studied the Pomo and commented on their distinctive basketry in 1919:

> *Pomo baskets have the name according to many of being the finest in the world. Evidently basket manufacture is no mere utilitarian routine to them, in which they have settled into mechanical habits like other tribes, but an art, the mastery of which is a stimulus and whose possibilities are played with. The height of this display is reached in the basket whose entire exterior is a mass of feathers perhaps with patterns in 2 or 3 lustrous colors. To the Pomo, these served as gifts and treasures, and above all, they were destroyed in honor of the dead. It is impressive and representative of the gently melancholy sentiments of the Pomo that these specimens of the highest artistic achievement of their civilization were dedicated to the purposes of mourning their kindred.*[1]

1. Quoted in "Pomo Baskets for Gifts and Ceremonies." www.kstrom.net/isk/art/basket/pomo.html.

These Pomo baskets with magnesite beads used for decoration were photographed in the 1920s.

Columbia and the Fraser Rivers were full of salmon, which the Native Americans captured as the fish traveled in large numbers to spawn each year. A wide variety of fishing methods was used, including lines with bone hooks, nets, spears, harpoons, nooses, and wooden traps. Berries, roots, and bulbs were prevalent in their diet as well.

Diversity in California

Lying directly west of the Great Basin and south of the Northwest Coast region is California, itself composed of numerous subregions, each with a distinctive microenvironment. Many of these habitats possess plentiful natural resources. This attracted early migrating people to the region and stimulated population growth among those who settled there. "Aboriginal California was biotically rich, densely populated, and culturally diverse," stated former University of Oregon professor Melvin Aikens, "more so than any comparable area of North America."[21]

The tremendous diversity of the California Native American cultures, among them the Wintun, Yuki, Miwok, Pomo, Kato, Chumash, and Chilula, can be seen in the wide array of food sources they enjoyed. Native Americans in California's southeastern deserts survived on mesquite (small spiny trees and bushes in the pea family), beans, and cactus fruits; inhabitants of the semi-forested central valleys hunted deer and small game and gathered acorns; people living along the coast caught seals and fish and collected shellfish; and mountain peoples hunted deer and wild goats and gathered pine nuts. Also, some primitive planting strategies developed in central California, where they raised oaks to produce acorns and cultivated prickly pear cactus to obtain its fruit.

For reasons that are unclear, the early Native American peoples of California did not develop strong political organization and wealth-based social divisions as did their neighbors on the northern coasts. Instead, most California peoples broke down into subtribal units, each consisting of from a hundred to a few thousand people. Modern scholars sometimes describe these units as "tribelets." "There was a high degree of isolation among different tribelets," researcher Carl Waldman pointed out, "with little movement of peoples once the group was established."[22] This unique social structure apparently discouraged warfare such as that seen in many other parts of North America. Although some conflicts must have arisen from time to time, the California communities generally coexisted in peace.

During these long periods of peace, various California Native American communities developed craft skills of an extremely high level. Of particular note were the baskets woven by the Pomo, who lived in the area north of San Francisco Bay. These artifacts rank among the most beautiful examples of that art from any society in world history. Fortunately, the intricate techniques involved passed from generation to generation among Pomo women, and their descendants are still producing magnificent baskets in the 21st century.

Residents of the Southwest

Strong craft skills and traditions also developed in the Southwest, the region lying east of southern California and including what are now Arizona, New Mexico, and parts of neighboring states. In this region, the leading craft was ceramics, or pottery making. Most of the southwestern peoples made pottery by manipulating wet clay and then using either sunlight or fire to harden it. They painted the hardened clay with brushes made from the fibers of the yucca plant. Especially impressive were the ceramic containers made by the Mogollon peoples of New Mexico's Mimbres River valley.

The region in which these and neighboring groups lived was and remains arid and rugged. Terrains range from flat, hot deserts in the South to high, windswept plateaus in the North, punctuated in various places by deep canyons and clusters of stony mountains. As was the case with other Archaic Native Americans, the residents of this region were hunter-gatherers at first. However, in time they developed a large-scale agricultural system that produced huge quantities of maize, beans, and squash. Several of the local groups also grew cotton and used the fibers to make clothes. Among

These bowls were made by artisans who lived in the Mimbres River Valley between 1000 and 1150.

these peoples were the Havasupai (who lived inside the Grand Canyon), Walapai, Yuma, Pima, Mojave, Hopi, Hohokam, and Zuni. The Apache and Navajo arrived much later than the others after migrating from the North.

Scholars suspect that some of these southwestern groups, including the Hopi, were descended from a very successful earlier people. They are most often referred to today as the Ancestral Puebloans. The Ancestral Puebloans lived atop the region's northern plateau (in the so-called Four Corners area) in late Archaic times and developed effective farming techniques, including elaborate irrigation systems that diverted water from rivers and creeks to fields. For reasons still not well understood, their numbers increased substantially after AD 700. For several centuries, they enjoyed increasing prosperity.

At first the Ancestral Puebloans lived in pit houses, which were round structures partly buried underground, with dome-shaped roofs made of wattle. People entered through a hole in the ceiling and climbed down a ladder. Over time they expanded these dwellings by adding walls made of adobe (mud brick) aboveground. Houses, storerooms, and communal centers (large round chambers called kivas) grew more numerous and interconnected until they formed a large complex called a pueblo. The builders grouped "the rooms together with shared walls and on top of one another, ladders connecting the various levels," Waldman explained. "With the levels stepped back in terraces, the roofs of one could serve as the front yards of another below."[23]

The golden age of the pueblos roughly spanned the period of 1100 to 1300. The Ancestral Puebloans became extremely prosperous, and their techniques of building, farming, weaving, and pottery making spread outward across neighboring areas of the Southwest. Pueblo society was highly dependent on farming, especially growing corn to feed its large population. Religious rites were a vital aspect of their culture, and elaborate religious rituals evolved to ensure sufficient rain and abundant harvests. According to Gibson,

> *The annual opening of the irrigation ditches, the harvest, rain-making pageants—all were occasions for*

pueblo religious observance. It is estimated that pueblo men spent at least half of their time in religious activities. Some were private … rites in the kivas. Some were public ceremonies with colorful costumes, ritual dancing, and chanting.[24]

In the 1200s, the Ancestral Puebloans suddenly abandoned their pueblos, including many of their possessions, and moved southward and eastward. Some scholars think a 30-year drought that started in 1270 adversely affected the crops. Other theories for this population displacement include soil erosion or

The pueblos built by the Ancestral Puebloans influenced the building styles of many Native American groups who came after them.

Common Religious Ideas

The details of Native American religion vary between regions and groups. They "had different views of the supernatural world," New York State Historical Association researcher Carl Waldman pointed out, "with varying types of deities and spirits ... lore concerning the creation and structure of the universe; [and] an array of rites, ceremonies, and sacred objects."[1] However, most Native American groups did have certain basic religious ideas in common. For example, according to University of Oklahoma scholar Arrell M. Gibson, their "universe was directed by an omnipotent creative-directive force, and the physical environment was alive with various spirits, good and bad, which had to be placated [appeased] in order to succeed in various enterprises. One's clan association provided a supernatural link with an animal ancestor, which related one to all living things."[2] Waldman added: "Shamanism was a common form of religious practice, in which individuals sought to control these spirits through the use of magic."[3] Other similarities between Native American religions included "the vision quests [to make contact with the spirits], and the use of psychotropic [mind-altering] plants to facilitate those visions; music and dance as a part of ritual; and the notion of sacrifice to gain the favor of the gods or spirits."[4]

1. Carl Waldman, *Atlas of the North American Indian*. New York, NY: Facts On File, 1985, p. 57.

2. Arrel M. Gibson, *The American Indian: Prehistory to the Present*. Lexington, MA: D.C. Heath, 1980, pp. 54–55.

3. Carl Waldman, *Atlas of the North American Indian*, p. 57.

4. Carl Waldman, *Atlas of the North American Indian*, p. 57.

deforestation; invasions of warlike intruders, perhaps some of the Utes, Navajos, or Apache peoples; or a combination of these factors.

Later, other tribes, including the Hopi, built pueblos in the region. (Hence, they are sometimes called Pueblo Peoples.) They grew corn, beans, pumpkins, and other crops. The Hopi pueblo at Oraibi in northeastern Arizona, still in use today, is the longest continually occupied settlement in the United States. It stands as a testament to the era when the American southwest supported one of the world's most accomplished and successful premodern civilizations.

Chapter Four

NATIVE AMERICANS OF THE GREAT PLAINS

The Great Plains stretch over 500 miles (800 km) east to west from the Missouri River to the Rocky Mountains, and more than 1,800 miles (2,900 km) north to south from the Rio Grande River to the Mackenzie River in Canada. As the United States grew, the land was divided into the states of Colorado, Kansas, Montana, Nebraska, North Dakota, Oklahoma, South Dakota, Texas, Wyoming, and parts of New Mexico. The Canadian provinces of Alberta, Manitoba, Saskatchewan, and parts of the Northwest Territory are included as well.

The tall and medium grasses supported many large animal species, including white-tailed deer, antelopes, elk, bighorn sheep, moose, and pronghorn. Smaller prairie dogs, coyotes, lynx, and gray or timber wolves thrived as well. Insects, including locusts and chiggers, were abundant. Millions of bison roamed and grazed on these immense grasslands.

The Mandan, Hidatsa, and other Native Americans had a large presence on the Great Plains. According to O'Brien,

> *Their towns became major centers of trade as buffalo hunters exchanged robes and meat for crops, baskets, and other products. Pawnees … relied on a mixed agricultural and buffalo-hunting culture that melded with their belief system so that corn harvests and buffalo hunts depended on each other for success.*

> *In the centuries before European contact, the plains were a dynamic place characterized by migrating buffalo herds, agriculture along the rivers, and the movement of peoples in and out … Siouan-speaking peoples, such as the Kansas, Otos, Missouris, Poncas, and Omahas, migrated into*

the plains from the East and tended to combine agriculture with buffalo hunting ... This configuration of peoples on the plains was still changing when the Europeans arrived, and it altered again because of European intrusion and the introduction of ... horses.[25]

Improved Hunting Techniques

Throughout the Paleo and Archaic periods, hunts for bison, elk, antelope, and other large mammals were conducted on foot. One common early hunting method for bison was the foot surround. It consisted of a long line of people who encircled a group of grazing bison and slowly tightened the circle. After two, three, or more of the animals were surrounded, hunters killed them with spears.

Improvements in such basic techniques, as well as in the effectiveness of hunting weapons, appeared only very slowly and gradually. However, each improvement made it easier to kill large prey, which sustained existing hunting societies and promoted further exploitation of the region by both them and newcomers. For example, in the late Archaic period, bison corrals came into use. Several animals could be herded into a corral, or pound, and killed later at the hunters' convenience. What archaeologists call the Ruby corral site, located on a tributary of the Powder River in Wyoming, is an excellent example. "The corral bears a surprising resemblance to modern cattle corrals," Fagan wrote.

The hunters erected pairs of stout posts separated by the diameter of the horizontal timbers wedged between them.

The native peoples of the Great Plains depended on bison for their survival.

The result was a strong structure that could withstand the onslaught [attack] of penned animals ... Excavators found bison ribs and jaws that were used for digging the post holes into the soft, sandy soil. The builders used juniper wood, perhaps burning off suitable poles rather than cutting them down ... Twenty hunters could have taken between 10 and 14 days to build the Ruby corral.[26]

Another hunting improvement, the Besant point, appeared on the Great Plains in about 300 BC. When used with the atlatl, this long, side-notched point was more effective against bison than earlier points. Another important weaponry advance was the bow and arrow, which came into use on the Great Plains in about AD 500. At first it merely supplemented spears and atlatls. However, over time a number of Native American groups made the bow their chief hunting weapon. Its advantages were that arrows shot from bows traveled farther than spears or shafts fired by atlatls, arrows were easier to make and lighter to carry than spears, many arrows could be carried by a single hunter, and arrows were easier and faster to load onto a bow than pointed shafts were onto a spear. Overall, the construction of the bow and arrow had a clever design:

The construction of the bow and arrows used by the Native Americans was clever. The physics depended a great deal on the length and weight of all the materials involved in the bow and arrows. While the natives may not have understood the concept of

This image shows Native American hunters using a spear and a bow and arrow to down a bison.

physics and trajectory, they definitely mastered the practical aspects of it.[27]

Still another hunting improvement was an increased use of an old strategy that had been employed when possible and practical since late Ice Age times. Later called the bison jump, it consisted of a band of hunters stampeding a group of bison over a steep bluff or small cliff. Because dozens or even hundreds of the beasts were killed in such a communal hunt, plains hunters probably conducted them infrequently, when certain conditions seemed to warrant them.

Many of these bison hunters eventually settled down in semipermanent camps. Most of these settlements were located in the low hills along the western borders of the plains rather than on the grasslands themselves. Commonly, bands of hunters ventured out onto the plains in the summer and fall, which was when the bison formed large herds. One good hunt could provide enough bison to meet a settlement's needs for many months.

The Plains Woodland Native Americans

However, by the time the bow and arrow appeared, some of these western Great Plains bison hunters regularly killed more beasts than they actually needed to sustain themselves. They traded the extra carcasses to other Native Americans living in the eastern sector of the Great Plains. These eastern Great Plains peoples are often called the Plains Woodland Native Americans. (They are also sometimes referred to as the Plains Village Native Americans because they generally lived in permanent villages.) In exchange for the dead bison, they gave their western neighbors bushels of corn, beans, and squash. These crops were the mainstay of the Great Plains Woodland Native Americans' diet. They did eat some bison meat, but only as a supplement to vegetables; and they sought the bison carcasses mainly for the hides, sinew (tendon), and bones, which they used for making clothes and tools.

Who were these Great Plains farmers and where did they come from? The answer seems to be that most, including the Mandan, Hidasta, Caddo, Wichita, and Pawnee, had descended from the same Archaic peoples the western Great Plains Native Americans had. Thus, the eastern Great Plains peoples had originally been bison hunters who supplemented their diets by foraging for roots, berries, seeds, and other plant products. By AD 850, however, knowledge of agriculture filtered into their homelands. In the centuries that followed, these groups largely replaced hunting with farming. It eventually became typical for a single Native American farming family to produce between 10 to 20 large bushels of maize, beans, squash, and sunflowers per season.

The need to tend and nurture their farming plots on a nearly full-time basis forced these peoples to create permanent villages. These villages often housed a thousand or more people. Women generally tended the fields, using hoes and

Once food sources became more consistent through agriculture and improved hunting techniques, formerly nomadic groups built more permanent settlements.

rakes made of elk or bison shoulder blades. The men did any necessary fishing or hunting.

Still another shared trait of the Great Plains farmers was the use of permanent dwellings, including the tepee, or tipi. A family of up to 10 people might live in one of these cone-shaped tents made of bison skin. According to one account,

> *Some tipi covers were painted … Designs included geometric shapes, sacred animals important to the designer, legends, and battle scenes. Women usually made, erected, dismantled, and maintained tipis, but men painted the designs, and the overall design was exclusive to the painter. The Kiowas … and the Blackfeet … were particularly renowned for their painted tipis.*[28]

In the Upper Missouri River Valley, the Mandan, Hidatsa, and Arikara people built earth lodges, or *awahte*. They were between 40 to 60 feet (12 to 18 m) in diameter and 10 to 15 feet (3 to 4 m) high. The construction was done mostly by the women, in about 10 days. Between 10 to 20 people lived in each earth lodge. They slept in raised beds around the perimeter of the lodge. A fire pit in the center was used for cooking, with smoke going through a hole in the ceiling. Residents sat on the mats around the pit, with the oldest male or a respected visitor using a raised seat called an *atuka*. Cache pits in the floor and outside of the earth lodge stored food and goods. The earth lodge was a sacred structure, often containing a small shrine near the back.

These farmers rarely moved around. However, on occasion, during periods of drought when harvests were poor, they sent out bands of hunters to catch big animals, especially bison. Like other Great Plains peoples, they transported loads of supplies and dead beasts on pole sledges pulled by teams of dogs. In 1598, a Spanish explorer visited the southern Great Plains and saw these dogs in action. They were "medium sized, shaggy dogs," he later wrote,

> *which they harness like mules. They have large droves of them, each girt around the breast and haunches, carrying a load of at least one hundred pounds ... They travel at the same pace as their masters. It is both interesting and amusing to see them traveling along, one after the other, dragging the ends of their poles.*[29]

Horses Affect the Culture

Much of the lifestyle changed when the first horses appeared on the Great Plains. The Spanish brought horses with them in the 1500s when they began exploring New Mexico in the Southwest. As the Spanish came into contact with different Native American groups more frequently, those Native Americans were introduced to the horses the Spanish had with them. Over time, these Native Americans began using horses themselves, and these animals had a huge impact on the lifestyles of groups living in the Southwest and the Great Plains, such as the Ute people, who became famous for their riding ability.

The southwestern Native Americans swiftly learned to care for, breed, and ride the horses, and they began to pass on this knowledge to neighboring tribes. Before ever meeting settlers, increasing numbers of Great Plains Indians heard about the fabulous "mystery dogs," or "sacred dogs" as they initially referred to horses. Horse breeding and the creation of new herds spread onto the Great Plains. The Apache, who were still in the process of migrating toward the Southwest, had horses at least by 1640. The Comanche in northern Texas had them by 1700; the Shoshone in Wyoming had them by 1720; the western Great Plains Cheyenne, Arapaho, Crow, Blackfeet, and Sioux had them by 1740; and the Assiniboin and Cree of the far northern Great Plains had them only a decade or two later.

The horse transformed the lives of these peoples. "With horses," Texas Tech University professor Paul H. Carlson explained,

> *they could take more bison and animal skins to exchange with traders for blankets, beads, knives, hatchets, [and so on]. Moreover, horses became a significant element in gift-giving— important in plains Indians' concepts of status and rank. Horse ownership became a symbol of a man's skill and bravery, for he had to acquire horses by raiding the enemy or by capturing them in the wild. In short, the horse became the most important vehicle of transportation, medium of exchange, and regulator of economic values and social status. It came to exercise*

By using horses to hunt, Native Americans could more consistently find and kill bison and other animals.

> *considerable influence over the minds of the people, altering world views, religious practices, subsistence patterns, and even the traditional nature and ideology of warfare.*[30]

The manner in which horses altered food acquisition and lifestyles on the Great Plains was particularly striking. Some of the farmers of the eastern Great Plains, such as the Mandan, retained their fields and crops. However, others, including the Pawnee, largely gave up farming and adopted a nomadic existence as mounted bison hunters. Meanwhile, many western Great Plains groups that had long dwelled on the edges of the vast grasslands now moved out onto the Great Plains and, like the Pawnee, became nomads following the herds.

Development of the Horse and Bison Culture

As time went on, these nomadic hunters exchanged ideas and copied one another's customs. Techniques of hunting with the bow and arrow from a moving horse, for example, became the same across the Great Plains. Also, nearly all the nomadic groups in the region started to use tepees, which ensured a group's mobility. In addition, everyone's transport sledges were now pulled by horses rather than by dogs. Therefore, a sharing of customs and a sort of blending of Great Plains

Artful Horsemanship

Some plains warriors developed horse riding to a level far beyond that ever achieved by Europeans. In his 19th-century travels on the Great Plains, noted painter and writer George Catlin observed the amazing riding skills of Comanche warriors, later calling them "the most extraordinary horsemen that I have yet seen in all my travels." According to Catlin's riveting account:

> *Amongst their feats of riding, there is one that has astonished me more than anything of the kind I have ever seen, or expect to see, in my life … by which [a young man] is able to drop his body upon the side of his horse at the instant he is passing, effectually screened from his enemies' weapons as he lays in a horizontal position behind the body of his horse, with his heel hanging over the horse's back; by which he has the power of throwing himself up again, and changing to the other side of the horse if necessary. In this wonderful condition, he will hang whilst his horse is at fullest speed, carrying with him his bow and his shield, and also his long lance of fourteen feet in length, all or either of which he will wield upon his enemy as he passes; rising and throwing his arrows over the horse's back, or with equal ease and equal success under the horse's neck.*[1]

1. George Catlin, *Letters and Notes on the Manners, Customs, and Conditions of North American Indians, vol. 1.* New York, NY: Dover, 1973, p. 321.

Comanche warriors were well known for their extraordinary skill on horseback.

New Animal, New Possibilities

As National Geographic writer David Quammen explained in his documentary *People of the Horse*, the arrival and use of the horse changed the culture and the balance of power for the Native Americans of the Great Plains:

> *Horses had opened new possibilities. They allowed men to hunt buffalo more productively than ever before, to range farther, to make devastating raids against other tribes. They relieved women of some onerous duties, such as lugging possessions from camp to camp. They tipped the balance, in population growth and territorial expansion, between hunting tribes and farming tribes, favoring the former. They also replaced the only previously domesticated animal in North America, the dog, which was much smaller and weaker and had to be fed meat. A horse could live off the land, eating what people and dogs didn't want: grass. When drought or winter snows made grass unavailable, it could even survive on cottonwood bark.*
>
> *The new animals were so prized that they began to fill a more abstract cultural role: as accrued wealth. If a man was savvy, ambitious, and lucky, he could amass a large herd; his excess horses could then be sold or traded or given away (in exchange for heightened prestige) or, if he let his guard down, stolen. Accrued wealth ushered in social stratification, and for the first time on the Plains there were rich Indians and poor Indians.*[1]

1. David Quammen, *National Geographic Magazine*, "People of the Horse." ngm.nationalgeographic.com/2014/03/horse-tribes/quammen-text.

cultures occurred in the 1700s and early 1800s. Modern scholars sometimes call the resulting mixture the Composite Plains Culture, although it is more often referred to as the Horse and Bison Culture.

Another cultural aspect that became increasingly similar across the Great Plains was a set of religious rituals that revolved around supernatural visions experienced by individuals. The belief was that in an altered mental state a person might receive guidance from ancestral spirits. The warrior kept a medicine bag or bundle that included items of spiritual importance, such as arrowheads, beads, horse hair, or rocks.

One cultural trait that individual groups of the Horse and Bison Culture did not share was language. Each

Selective Hunting

While excavating a bison kill site at Garnsey, New Mexico, archaeologist John Speth of the University of Michigan discovered that Native American hunters were extremely observant about the physical attributes of their prey and often did not kill bison and other beasts indiscriminately. In the kill he examined, the hunters were selective and went after the male bison. Speth thinks this was because the males are hardier in the spring and that their bone marrow has a higher fat content than that of females at that time of year. The Native Americans may have preferred fattier meat because it is an important source of energy and certain nutrients.

group retained its original spoken tongue. Yet these groups frequently came into contact and needed to communicate with one another. So they developed a sign language consisting primarily of hand gestures.

In explaining the importance of the sign language, Dr. Jeffrey E. Davis explained,

> *American Indian nations of the Great Plains and cultural groups bordering this geographic area spoke so many different languages that verbal communication between them was difficult. As extensive trade networks developed and political alliances became necessary, an elegant language of the hands developed that cut across spoken language barriers. Though now endangered, this sign language continues to serve a vital role in traditional storytelling, rituals, legends, prayers, conversational narratives, and as a primary language of American Indians who are deaf.*[31]

Some of the first European explorers who visited the region mistakenly assumed that this sign language had predated the area's spoken languages. However, the truth was completely the opposite. This was only one of many misunderstandings and cultural differences between the Native Americans and settlers that would eventually lead all the Great Plains Groups to the brink of extinction.

Chapter Five

EARLY NATIVE AMERICANS OF THE SOUTHEAST

The vast Southeast region included Louisiana, Mississippi, Alabama, and Florida along the Gulf of Mexico, as well as Georgia and Tennessee to the North. Some aspects of southeastern Native American culture also extended into the Carolinas, Virginia, and the Ohio River valley. (The peoples of the Ohio Valley were culturally related to the northeastern Native Americans as well. In fact, archaeologists often group a number of northeastern and southeastern Native American groups together under the label "Eastern Woodlands" Native Americans.)

The Mississippian Era

In the late Archaic Era, also known as the Mississippian Era (from about AD 700 to 1500), a new civilization developed. The people cleared fields to plant crops. There is archaeological evidence of large political-territorial units, each with a central town. The community had a societal hierarchy and followed matrilineal kinship. In addition, a high-ranking chief ruled each group. These chiefdoms varied in size from a small village to several cities and additional suburban-like groups.

One common characteristic of these new groups was that they erected earthen mounds. Many of these mounds were used as burial sites. In some towns, especially in the later years of the Mississippian Era, the ruling elite built their houses on top of the highest mounds, and then used the mounds as their burial sites. Evidence of what researchers believe were the most important towns has been found at Cahokia in southeastern Illinois, Moundville in western Alabama, Cofitachequi in western South Carolina, and Coosa in northern Alabama.

The Mississippian civilization, which lasted for some 2,500 years, was an

Earthen mounds were used as burial sites and as gathering places for ceremonies.

intermediary stage between the Archaic Native Americans of the Southeast and the many localized groups that formed there after the decline of the large chiefdoms. Many of these southeastern groups retained the important political, social, and religious customs of the mysterious Mound Builders.

Just prior to the arrival of European settlers in North America, many separate groups inhabited the vast Southeast. Among them were the Creeks, Choctaw, Seminole, Cherokee, Chickasaw, Tuskegee, Cusabo, Natchez, and Alabama. Although these groups occupied numerous different terrains and ecological niches within the Southeast, they all experienced certain similar geographic and climatic conditions. As a whole, the area is well watered, with plentiful rainfall and rich soil, for instance. It also features many low mountain ranges (the largest being the Appalachians) with rolling hills, deep forests, and numerous river valleys. The local Native Americans lived mostly in permanent villages in these valleys. The vast majority of them were farmers who supplemented their diets by fishing, hunting, and foraging.

The Mound-Building Civilization

Most early European explorers lacked a true appreciation for the number and size of the earthworks erected by the Mound Builders. Only when European civilization began to spread westward from the eastern seaboard in the late 1700s and early 1800s did settlers realize the vast extent and achievements of the mound-building civilization. One of the first writings that called attention to the Mound Builders was Thomas Jefferson's *Notes on the State of Virginia*, which was published in 1785. Besides being one of the founding fathers of the United States, Jefferson was a versatile individual with interests and broad knowledge in many scholarly disciplines. He was particularly fascinated by Native Americans and their origins and customs, and he personally excavated a small ancient

A Burial Mound at the Rivanna River

The American patriot and third U.S. president, Thomas Jefferson, was fascinated by Native Americans and their history. In 1782 he excavated a burial mound not far from his Virginia home and later described it:

> *There being one of these [mounds] in my neighbourhood ... I determined to open and examine it thoroughly. It was situated on the low grounds of the Rivanna [River], about two miles above its principal fork, and opposite to some hills, on which had been an Indian town. It was of a spherical form, of about 40 feet diameter at the base, and had been of about twelve feet altitude [height], though now reduced by the plow to seven and a half feet ... I first dug superficially in several parts of it, and came to collections of human bones, at different depths, from six inches to three feet below the surface. These were lying in the utmost confusion, some vertical, some oblique, some horizontal, and ... entangled, and held together in clusters by the earth ... The bones of which the greatest numbers remained were skulls, jaw-bones, teeth, the bones of the arms, thighs, legs, feet, and hands.*[1]

1. Thomas Jefferson, *Notes on the State of Virginia,* American Studies at the University of Virginia. xroads.virginia.edu/~hyper/JEFFERSON/ch11.html.

Indian mound in his native Virginia. The mounds, he wrote,

> *are of different sizes, some of them constructed of earth, and some of loose stones. That they were repositories of the dead, has been obvious to all ... Some have thought they covered the bones of those who have fallen in battles ... Some ascribed them to the custom, said to prevail among the Indians, of collecting, at certain periods, the bones of all their dead ... Others again supposed them the general [cemeteries] for towns.*[32]

Jefferson did not venture a guess about who had built these mounds. He seems to have assumed that ancient Native Americans had done so, an opinion that was summarily dismissed by the next generation of scholars who studied the mounds. Indeed, in the nineteenth century most whites concluded that these large-scale mounds, especially those 30 feet (9 m), 50 feet (15 m), and even 100 feet (30.5

m) tall, could not be the work of Native Americans. As James A. Brown of Northwestern University stated:

> *The then prevalent white attitude [was] that Native Americans were too indifferent to labor to have been capable of devoting the effort required in the mounds' construction and would not have had the engineering knowledge to plan and execute the most demanding examples. So entrenched were early [white] Americans in their negative perception of Native American abilities that they paid little attention to any testimony to the contrary.*[33]

The testimony that seemed more believable to non-Native American researchers and writers was that the mounds had been erected by a lost race of whites. The most popular theory was that members of the so-called lost tribes of Israel had erected the mounds. When one educated observer, James McCulloh, argued that the Native Americans' own ancestors had done it, he was ignored or ridiculed.

McCulloh was finally proven right when the newly created federal Bureau of American Ethnology thoroughly investigated numerous mounds across the Southeast between 1881 and 1893. This study, headed by scholar Cyrus Thomas, showed conclusively that the mounds had been built by the not-too-distant ancestors of various Native American groups in the region. Thus, one important part of the mystery of the Mound Builders had been solved.

Mound Builders at Poverty Point and Adena

The first mounds in the Southeast were likely small piles of earth, each intended to inter a single warrior or chief. Due to erosion from rain, wind, floods, and other natural processes, most of these initial mounds are either gone or will never be found. Therefore, archaeologists remain unsure when and where the first mounds were erected.

However, they all agree that the earliest large-scale example was at Poverty Point, near the confluence of the Arkansas and Mississippi rivers in northern Louisiana. Poverty Point, which flourished roughly between 1750 and 1350 BC, seems to have been a well-organized town shaped like a hemisphere, or giant C. Following the natural curve of the hemisphere are 6 concentric earthen ridges that measure, on average, 10 feet (3 m) tall and 82 feet (25 m) wide. They were originally higher and may have supported rows of wooden or wattle houses.

To the West of these ridges lies a huge mound some 72 feet (21.9 m) tall and more than 660 feet (200 m) long. The purpose of this mound is uncertain. No human remains have been found in it, so it does not appear to have been for burials. Tools, artifacts, and stones found there have led archaeologists to surmise that Poverty Point may have been a regional trading center.

Overall, the most striking thing about Poverty Point is its unusual size and layout. Its building required a massive amount of organization and cooperation

The Poverty Point Settlement

The reason the builders of Poverty Point, in northern Louisiana, chose that particular spot is unknown. However, the late geologist and archaeologist Roger Saucier ventured this guess:

I guess we'll probably never know exactly why [the] Poverty Point people settled exactly where they did. I have a feeling that that is probably largely a matter of socio-economics or perhaps a socio-political factor. But obviously the Poverty Point peoples liked the margins of ridges like Macon Ridge. This has afforded them high ground relatively immune from flooding, with good arable soils and good locations for living conditions. But perhaps more importantly, this enabled them to be immediately adjacent to these very rich bottomland forests and hardwood areas that are so abundant as far as plants and wildlife and fisheries are concerned.[1]

1. Quoted in Louisiana Office of State Parks, "Poverty Point Earthworks: Evolutionary Milestones of the Americas." www.lpb.org/programs/povertypoint/pp_transcript.html.

This aerial view shows the layout of the ancient village of Poverty Point in northern Louisiana. Notice the ancient mounds.

in an age when other Native Americans in the region were living in tiny, primitive villages. O'Brien explained, "Its localized power extended outward when labor from surrounding communities, either coerced or voluntary, was used to build the various structures. Social ranking also existed at Poverty Point, as shown through certain rare, elite items found only in burial mounds at one location by the largest mound."[34]

Though their town was highly unique for its time, the residents of Poverty Point sustained themselves as other southeastern Native Americans did—through hunting, fishing, and foraging, supplemented by a little farming. The same was true of the next major group of Mound Builders in the region, called the Adena culture. It was the first mound-building society that spread outward and encompassed numerous settlements in a wide area. Centered in southern Ohio, Adena sites have been found in Kentucky and other nearby states. The Adena culture thrived from about 500 BC to about AD 100.

Unlike the Poverty Point earthworks, the dome- or cone-shaped Adena mounds in Indiana, Kentucky, West Virginia, and Pennsylvania were used mainly for burial. Some travelers also used them as landmarks. Generally such a mound began when an honored person was buried in a shallow pit and people poured basketfuls of earth over the grave to mark it. Then, over time, other burials were placed atop the bottom one and as a result the mound grew larger and larger. The Adena peoples also constructed non-burial earthworks that experts call effigy mounds. These are frequently shaped like animals, so they may have had religious significance. The most outstanding example is the Great Serpent Mound in Peebles, Ohio, shaped like an uncoiling snake and measuring 4 feet (1.2 m) high and 1,330 feet (405 m) long. An Adena mound in Chillicothe, Ohio, has recently been carbon dated to the first century AD.

The Hopewell Culture

During the last few centuries in which the Adena culture existed, another mound-building culture was rising to prominence in the Southeast. Modern scholars call this newer group of peoples the Hopewell culture, after the farm where artifacts were first found. It prospered from about 200 BC to roughly AD 500. Thus, during this historical overlap, both cultures coexisted for a while, though the extent and nature of their relationship is unclear.

More certain are that the Hopewells and Adenas were quite similar in a number of ways and that the Hopewell culture was based on Adena culture. However, the Hopewells created what might be called a more elaborate, mature, and spectacular version of Adena civilization. The Hopewells built more and larger mounds than the Adenas did, for example. Hopewell culture also spread over a much larger area, stretching from the Gulf of Mexico northward into the Great Lakes region. (Thus, the Hopewells influenced the cultures of a

Cahokia Suburb Discovered

In 2012, during a bridge construction project, archaeologists found the remains of a previously undiscovered Native American city. They unearthed over 1,000 houses and the base of a pyramid that had been buried under East St. Louis, Illinois, for hundreds of years. The researchers could only excavate part of the site, so they were not sure exactly how big the city was. They think the site covers all of the modern city of East St. Louis, and that it might have been a suburb of the nearby ancient city of Cahokia. Joe Galloy, the research coordinator, said:

> *One of the things that I imagine an ancient visitor to this site would have experienced was kind of a sense of awe and wonder. There would be fires and things like that. People cooking stuff—all sorts of activity. And you'd see this huge village. And it was probably a very impressive site, one of the largest settlements that people had seen if they hadn't been around this area before.*[1]

1. Quoted in Véronique LaCapra, "Ancient Suburb Near St. Louis Could Be Lost Forever," St. Louis Public Radio (transcript), June 2, 2012. news.stlpublicradio.org/post/ancient-suburb-near-st-louis-could-be-lost-forever#stream/0.

number of later northeastern groups, too.) The Hopewells also developed a more extensive agricultural system and more varied and impressive craft and artistic works.

The latter included copper earrings, breastplates, and deer, bird, and other animal figurines; pearl jewelry; obsidian knives and spearheads; small containers made from marine shells; figurines, mirrors, and geometric decorations made from thin sheets of mica; and new and differently-shaped pottery jars and bowls (in a style sometimes referred to as the Hopewell Series). These and many other artifacts were either manufactured in Hopewell towns or obtained through trade. Trade was especially important to the Hopewells, who exchanged goods with other peoples across nearly the entire eastern United States.

The most spectacular artifacts of Hopewell culture, however, were the many mounds its people erected. Often they were grouped in enormous complexes. At Chillicothe in the Ohio River valley, for instance, 38 mounds were built within an enclosure covering 110 acres (45 ha). At Newark, Ohio, a complex of mounds and other earthworks covers an area of more than 4 square miles (10.4 sq km). On average, the larger Hopewell mounds are some 30 feet (9 m) high and some are as tall as 100 feet (30.5 m).

The burial customs employed in these mounds varied. The type of grave, and the amount of goods placed in the grave, indicated some type of social structure. After performing various rituals, the mourners set the hut-like structures ablaze and then buried the remains beneath an earthen mound.

Central American Cultural Contacts

A number of archaeologists and other experts have pointed out certain similarities between the larger earthworks of the Mound Builders, especially those of the Mississippian phase, and the pyramids erected by the Maya, Aztec, and other Mesoamerican peoples. The latter, inhabiting what are now southern Mexico and some Central American countries, also had kings reminiscent of the great chiefs of the Mound Builders. So far, no connection has been found showing that Mesoamericans migrated to or visited the southeastern United States. However, some researchers have suggested an alternate scenario. Perhaps, they say, on a few occasions individuals from the Mound Builder cultures traveled to Mesoamerica and saw the cities and pyramids there. Returning home, they may have incorporated some of the architectural ideas they had witnessed into their own large-scale works. Other scholars find this idea unlikely and suggest that the peoples of the two regions developed these ideas independently.

(1) Cahokia Mounds

(2) Moundville

The Mississippian mound-building civilization dominated the American Southeast for around 800 years, with territories extending from the mouth of the White River in present-day Arkansas in the south, and eastward along the Ohio and Tennessee Rivers to what is now North Carolina, as the shaded areas of this map show.

The Mississippian Culture

Although archaeologists date the end of Hopewell culture and the beginning of the next mound-building civilization to about AD 500, the transition was probably not abrupt. It is possible that large-scale crop failures, intertribal wars, or some other disasters contributed to the Hopewell decline. However, the main reason for the rise of the next culture—which experts call the Mississippian—was likely fairly rapid adoption of new agricultural, social, and religious customs. In this way, Mississippian culture probably evolved from, rather than pushed aside and replaced, Hopewell culture.

A number of distinctive characteristics defined Mississippian culture, which dominated the Southeast for about 500 years. First, its people practiced intensive farming, particularly of corn, but also of beans, various gourds, and tobacco. (Tobacco was smoked, sniffed, or chewed in various religious ceremonies and also burned like incense or crushed and sprinkled in graves.) People still hunted and fished, but mainly as a supplement to agriculture.

The Mississippians also displayed a trend toward more centralized government and control of large expanses of territory. This new hierarchical political system had powerful chiefs, who belonged to certain family groups, and a more complex social structure with fairly rigid social classes. "These Indian groups," archaeologist Bruce D. Smith explained,

> *attained a sophisticated chiefdom level of socio-political organization. Such chiefdoms are characterized by the existence of a family or kin grouping enjoying elite social and political status. At the top of the hierarchy [social-political ladder] was the chief, who, along with a small group of closely related kinsmen, made many of the important decisions that faced the society.*[35]

The chiefs and other high-status individuals ate better foods and wore finer clothes than others. The latter not only grew the food and made the clothes but also provided the labor needed to raise the mounds utilized by the elite class. In fact, the manner in which Mississippian culture used its major mounds was another factor that set it apart from earlier mound-building societies. Some Mississippian mounds contained burials, like the Adena and Hopewell cultures did. However, the Mississippians erected temples and houses atop their bigger mounds. For this reason, archaeologists sometimes call their society the Temple Mound Builder culture. The temples were lodges made of wood, wattle, and earth, in which chiefs and other community leaders conducted public rituals. These Native American nobles also lived in lavish quarters built on top of the larger mounds and were buried in these same mounds.

The largest of the temple mounds, at Cahokia, near East St. Louis, Illinois, is 100 feet (30.5 m) high and covers

This is a side view of Monks Mound at Cahokia Mounds State Historic Site, Illinois. It is the largest man-made earthen mound in North America.

16 acres (6.4 ha). In its heyday, the Cahokia complex covered more than 5 square miles (12 sq km) and supported a population of more than 10,000. It seems to have been the capital of the most influential chiefdom in the Southeast, and its chief may have held sway over thousands of miles of territory.

The Mysterious Decline of the Mound Builders

The Cahokia chiefdom and other Native American mini-nations of the Southeast were gone by the time European settlers arrived in the region. The reasons for the decline of Mound Builders are unknown, and numerous theories have been advanced to explain it. Most likely, a number of factors—perhaps population decline, drought, climate change, crop failures, wars among chiefdoms, and so on—combined to break apart these peoples into the smaller units that the first settlers encountered.

In discussing what happened to the people, Pauketat wrote,

> *the facts … suggest that Cahokia was … made up of more than one ethnic group … Possibly, the people of Cahokia included local farmers*

Shown here is the Emerald Mound Site located in Mississippi.

and contingents of dignitaries and representatives from far-off peoples in the Plains, Midwest, and South. As Cahokia dissolved, the nonlocal citizens might have simply gone home. The descendants of Cahokians might include people in various tribal groups in the Plains and the South today.[36]

The Mound Builders of the Southeast were another example of a great Native American civilization that reached its peak and then declined shortly before first contact with European settlers.

Chapter Six

NATIVE AMERICANS OF THE NORTHEASTERN WOODLANDS

The Northeastern Woodlands region extended from just above the Great Lakes in Canada southward to Virginia. The area was bound by the Atlantic Ocean on the East and and the Ohio River on the West. The modern-day states of Maine, New Hampshire, Vermont, Massachusetts, Rhode Island, Connecticut, New York, Pennsylvania, New Jersey, and Virginia now cover the area. The region has several large rivers, including the Hudson, the Potomac, the Susquehanna, the Ohio, the Delaware, and the St. Lawrence. There are several low mountain ranges, including the Appalachians and the Catskills. There are many lakes and forests with abundant natural resources.

The Northern and Southern Algonquian

The Algonquian peoples, who were united by a shared language but spoke in different dialects, had the widest distribution of the Northeastern groups. In New England, for instance, the Micmac (in Maine), Massachuset and Wampanoag (in Massachusetts), and Narragansett (in Rhode Island) were Algonquians. So were the Ottawa (in northern Michigan), Montauk (in Long Island), and Delaware (in Delaware).

Researchers believe that sometime around AD 1000, groups of Haudenosaunee (commonly known as the Iroquois people) migrated northward from the Susquehanna River area in Maryland and Pennsylvania, and moved into territory in and around central and western New York. Since this area was already occupied by groups of Algonquian peoples, the Haudenosaunee move split the Algonquian territory into two parts. Some of the dialects and customs prevailed among the Huron (in Ontario), Mohawk and Seneca (in New York), and Tuscarora (originally in southern Virginia).

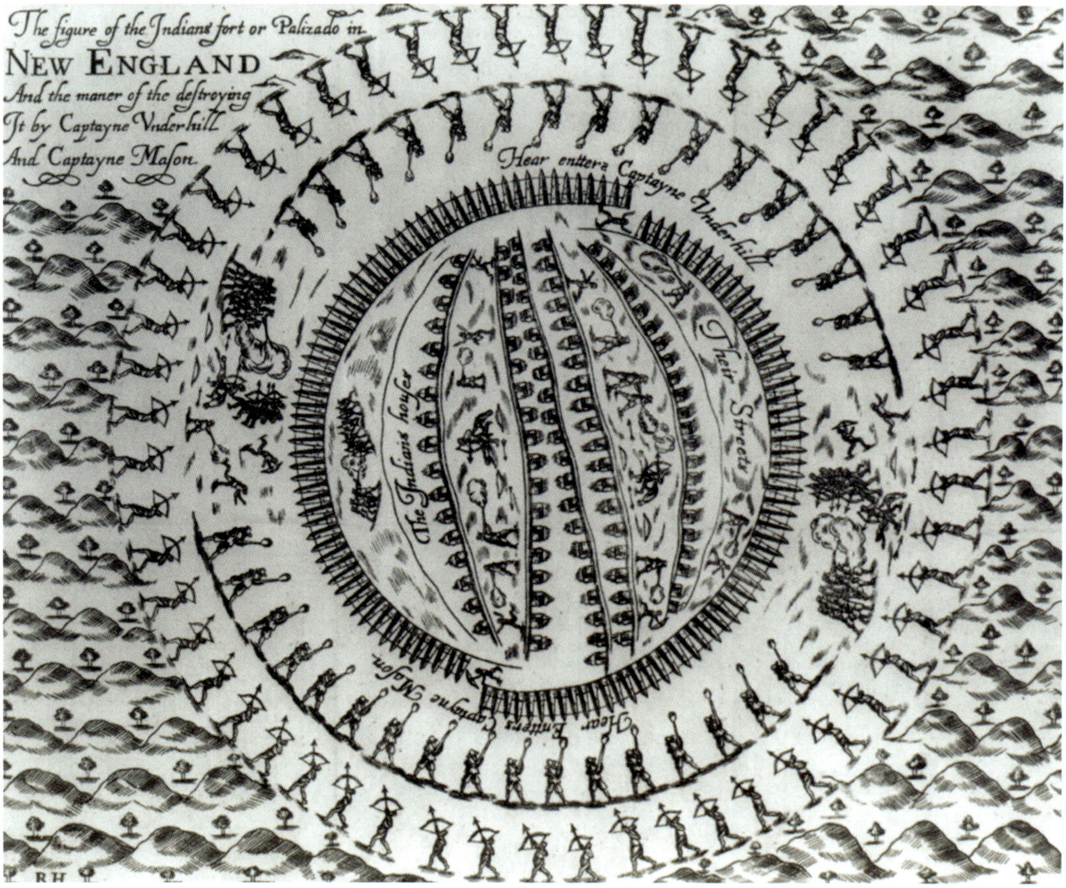

This artist's drawing shows a typical Pequot village. The Pequot people lived along the southeastern coast of Connecticut and Rhode Island, along the Pequot (now the Thames) and the Mystic Rivers.

Although the date for establishment is unclear, sometime around 1570, the Haudenosaunee established the Five Nations Iroquois Confederacy. The Mohawks, the Oneidas, the Onondagas, the Cayuga, and the Seneca were all original members; the Tuscarora joined in 1722, and the name was changed to Six Nations. The confederacy members pledged to remain peaceful within their group, and to defend all against outside enemies, including the Algonquian groups. It is interesting to note that the Algonquian word for Iroquois translates to "snake."

The establishment of the Haudenosaunee in New York, and also in the area north of Lake Ontario, more or less divided the Algonquins into two geographically separate groups. The northern Algonquians, based in southern Canada, retained an Archaic lifestyle up to and beyond contact with European settlers. These peoples of the deep northern forests hunted, fished, and foraged. They did not develop agriculture, possibly at least partially due to the cold climate. A typical band followed a circuit within a given territory, using canoes in the warm weather and snowshoes and toboggans in the winter. They hunted, fished, trapped, and foraged for wild plants. They used birch bark, to fashion storage containers, cooking utensils, and even canoes, and dressed in furs.

The so-called southern Algonquians, who inhabited New England, coastal New York and New Jersey, and Delaware, also hunted and fished. Those who lived near the ocean became adept at catching numerous animals that dwelled in estuaries and marshes (including various kinds of birds). As a result, they came to enjoy a diverse and rich diet. At a single site once occupied by a group of Massachuset, archaeologists found the remains of food sources that included fox, mink, bear, beaver, deer, harbor seal, blue heron, mallard duck, hawk, eagle, snapping turtle, scallops, quahogs, snails, clams, sea bass, stingray, and many more.

The southern Algonquians, unlike the northern Algonquians, supplemented their hunting, fishing, and foraging with farming. They grew corn, squash, beans, and tobacco. Generally, they soaked corn kernels in ashes, hulled them, and pounded the pulp to make hominy.

The Massachuset, Wampanoag, Nauset, and Narragansett all spoke the same Algonquian dialect, indicating that all of these groups were closely related. These and many other Algonquian groups not only shared a language and the same ways of acquiring food, they also had similar ways of governing themselves. For example, each local group was organized as a type of political unit called a sachemship. It was overseen by a chief-like individual known as a sachem.

This statue of Massasoit is in Plymouth, Massachusetts. Massasoit, also known as Ousemequin or Woosamenquen, was the sachem of the Wampanoags of New England in 1620 when the Pilgrims arrived. He successfully negotiated a peace treaty with the Pilgrims.

Always a male, he made decisions for the group about land use, trade, and warfare; aiding him in these deliberations was a handful of men, often distinguished warriors, each of whom also enjoyed higher-than-normal social rank.

Southern Algonquians also shared similar religious ideas that revolved around a spirit world. It was inhabited by various supernatural beings and forces, including the souls of deceased ancestors, collectively called manitou. Each community had a shaman (a combination of priest and magician), called a *pawauog*, who communicated with the manitou, generally through dreams or waking visions. In this way, the spirits could offer advice and guidance to ordinary folk.

Another custom common to southern Algonquians, as well as northern ones, was erecting their characteristic dwelling—the wigwam, which is the word for "house" in the Abenaki dialect. According to one expert:

> *The wigwam could be easily constructed in less than a day. The typical wigwam was oval and consisted of saplings set in the ground and bent into arches and lashed [together with plant fibers]. The resultant frame was covered with large bark strips ...*

Tribes that used wigwams similar to this one included the Massachuset, Nauset, and Narraganset.

leaving a smoke hole in the center and one end open for a doorway, which was covered with a hide or a woven rush [reed] mat ... The finished structure could be up to 20 feet long and 14 feet wide, with walls 6 or 7 feet high and an overall height of 14 feet at the arch. The sleeping areas were arranged around the central fire and consisted of mats or cedar boughs and animal skins.[37]

The Haudenosaunee

The most common dwellings of the Haudenosaunee were called longhouses because even average-sized ones were 50 to 100 feet (15 to 30.5 m) long; and some were exceptionally long—up to 300 feet (91.5 m), the length of a football field.

The frame of the Iroquois longhouse consisted of freshly cut young trees. The builders forced the bottoms of these saplings firmly into the ground and bent their tops over to form a curved ceiling. Then they covered the framework of this long, single room with thick layers of elm bark. There was a door on each end, which was covered with furs or hides in the winter.

On the outside, the longhouses were arranged in fairly tight groups, likely

A drawing of an Onondaga village shows the tight arrangement of longhouses, surrounded by a defensive stockade. A village could hold up to 3,000 people.

partly for mutual protection. However, further protection for the whole village was provided by a sturdy palisade (or stockade), a wooden perimeter wall made by lashing many small- and medium-sized tree trunks tightly together.

Although they were mainly farmers who stayed for many generations within fixed regions, the Haudenosaunee did periodically move around within these regions because of the manner in which they farmed—a technique now called slash and burn. A Haudenosaunee group or band first cleared an expanse of forest large enough to accommodate its village and fields. Then the people planted and harvested their crops for several seasons. However, as happens in farmland everywhere, over time the soil became depleted of nutrients, which severely reduced crop yields. Because they did not yet practice true crop rotation, after eight to ten years the Haudenosaunee farmers had to move on. They cleared a swath of forest a few miles away and started over, which necessitated building a new village. "Relocation," Kopper pointed out, "also shifted the population away from plagues of fleas and to new sources of firewood, vital for winter warmth."[38]

This firewood was burned inside the longhouses, where the villagers slept year-round and cooked, ate, and socialized in the cold months. A hearth was

This painting depicts typical daily activity inside an Iroquois longhouse.

The Role of Haudenosaunee Women

The New York State Museum provides this useful overview of the extended families and clans of the Haudenosaunee and the important roles that women played in them:

> *Longhouses have another thing in common besides their shape. They were built to serve as a home for a large extended family. An extended family includes a number of family units consisting of parents and children, plus grandparents, aunts, uncles, cousins, etc. In an Iroquois longhouse there may have been 20 or more families which were all related through the mothers' side, along with the other relatives. All these families belonged to the same clan; each clan in a village had its own longhouse; the clans had branches in other villages. Clans were named for animals and birds; Turtle, Bear, and Hawk are examples. The symbol for the clan was used in decorations of household objects, in tattoos, and on the front of the longhouse … The extended family not only shared the same building for their home, but they also worked together to make their living. The clan was the basic social and economic unit in Iroquois society and the leadership in the clans was through the women, because the kinship followed the mother's bloodline. The women managed the affairs of their longhouse, the farming, and distribution of food. They also selected the men who would represent their clan in the tribal council.*[1]

1. New York State Museum, "A Mohawk Iroquois Village." www.nysm.nysed.gov/IroquoisVillage/constructiontwo.html.

situated about every 20 feet (6 m) along a central aisle that ran down the middle of a longhouse. Generally two families shared each hearth, and members of these families slept on platforms raised above the floor on either side of the hearth. There were generally about 5 fires and 10 families in a longhouse.

The families were related because they were part of a larger kinship group—the clan. The Haudenosaunee followed a matrilineal line, which meant that members traced their ancestry back through the female, rather than the male, line. A clause of an important Haudenosaunee political document (originally preserved orally but later written down) states: "The lineal descent of the people … shall run in the female line. Women shall be considered the progenitors of the nation. They shall own the land and the soil. Men and women shall follow the status of the mother."[39]

The extended family, including grandparents, parents, siblings, and aunts and uncles, lived in a longhouse together. The clan mother was the head of the house. A new groom, who had to be from a different clan than his bride's, left his own longhouse and moved into her longhouse, which was overseen by the oldest female in her clan.

The Great Law of Peace

This matrilineal system was strictly social in nature. In the political realm, the Haudenosaunee chiefs who had charge of entire villages and groups were male. Another aspect of Haudenosaunee politics made it stand out from the politics of most other North American Native American groups. Namely, five of the major Haudenosaunee groups, all based in what is now New York State, came together in a major and long-lasting political alliance that the settlers called the Iroquois Confederacy. The member tribes—the Mohawk (People of the Flint), Oneida (People of the Standing Stone), Onondaga (People of the Hills), Cayuga (People of the Great Swamp), and Seneca (Great Hill People)—called themselves the Haudenosaunee, meaning "people who build a house." In 1722, two centuries after the arrival of the European settlers, a sixth tribe, the Tuscarora (Shirt-Wearing People), migrated to New York from North Carolina to escape the settlers, and joined the Confederacy.

The exact date and manner in which this famous league formed remain uncertain, however the estimate is that it was formed around 1570. As for how the alliance was formed, a founding story survived by word of mouth and was eventually written down.

The heroes of the story are the Peacemaker and his main supporter, a former Onondagan chief named Hiawatha. According to the legend, the Peacemaker asked the leaders of the five tribes to stop fighting one another and to live together in peace. When a feared Onondagan chief named Tadadaho opposed the idea,

> *the Peacemaker used arrows to demonstrate the strength of unity. First, he took a single arrow and broke it in half. Then he took five arrows and tied them together. This group of five arrows could not be broken. The Peacemaker said, "A single arrow is weak and easily broken. A bundle of arrows tied together cannot be broken. This represents the strength of having a confederacy. It is strong and cannot be broken."*[40]

The Confederacy had an organized plan for cooperation and defense. According to O'Brien,

> *The Senecas whose villages were located the farthest west in western New York and were the most*

The Hiawatha Belt shows the unity of the five founding nations of the Iroquois Confederacy. Left to right, the squares and tree represent the Seneca, the Cayuga, the Onondaga, the Oneida, and the Mohawk.

populous, became the "keepers of the western door," charged with protecting the confederacy from enemies in the Great Lakes area to the west. The Mohawks became known as the "keepers of the eastern door," guarding against any enemy incursions from the east. Each tribe had an equal vote in confederacy meetings. The Iroquois held all confederacy-wide council meetings among the Onondagas, whose villages were located in the geographical center of the confederacy and who, as the home of Hiawatha, provided the spiritual and political center of the confederacy. Each tribe sent civil chiefs appointed by clan mothers to the councils at Onondaga, and women played crucial political roles in selecting chiefs, determining whether or not to go to war, and deciding the fates of any captives seized in war from other peoples."[41]

The league proved to be highly successful because it was strong and bold enough to prevent wars among the tribes, but prudent and tactful enough to avoid intruding into the internal affairs of any one of them. "The confederacy was adaptive," Fagan wrote, "in that it allowed groups [of Haudenosaunee] to legislate against unnecessary blood feuding, while still maintaining individual cultural and political identity in their dealings with others."[42]

The key to this flexibility was a

The Uses and Importance of Wampum

Wampum, consisting of strands of decorative beads or shells, was used among the Iroquois and Algonquians to symbolize or conclude various important transactions or social or political events. The belts were not worn as clothing, nor used as money. This description of wampum comes from the constitution of the Iroquois Confederacy:

> *A bunch of shell strings is to be the symbol of the council fire of the Five Nations Confederacy. And the Lord whom the council of Fire Keepers shall appoint to speak for them in opening the council shall hold the strands of shells in his hands when speaking. When he finishes speaking he shall deposit the strings on an elevated place (or pole) so that all the assembled Lords and the people may see it and know that the council is open and in progress. When the council adjourns, the Lord who has been appointed by his comrade Lords to close it shall take the strands of shells in his hands and address the assembled Lords. Thus will the council adjourn until such time and place as appointed by the council. Then shall the shell strings be placed in a place for safekeeping.*[1]

1. Internet Modern History Sourcebook, "The Constitution of the Iroquois Confederacy," Fordham University. www.fordham.edu/halsall/mod/iroquois.html.

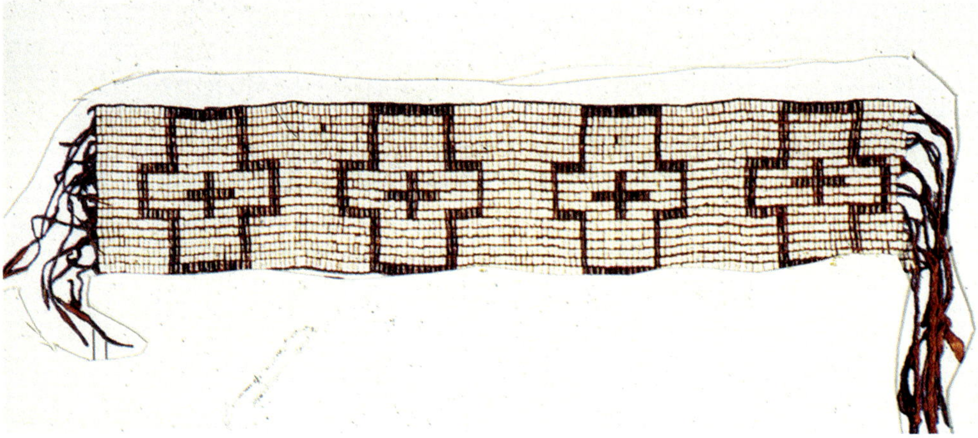

This wampum belt from around 1785 commemorated a peace treaty in the 18th century.

thoughtful and effective constitution, or set of legal rules and procedures, which still survives. The 117 articles of the Great Law of Peace calls for disputes to be decided by deliberation, discussion, and ultimately democratic voting among the member tribes. "First the question shall be [discussed and] passed upon by the Mohawk and Seneca Lords [league representatives]," one article states.

> *Then it shall be discussed and passed by the Oneida and Cayuga Lords. Their decisions shall then be referred to the Onondaga Lords ... for final judgment ... In all cases the procedure must be as follows. When the Mohawk and Seneca Lords have unanimously agreed upon a question, they shall report their decision to the Cayuga and Oneida Lords, who shall deliberate upon the question and report a unanimous decision to ... the Onondaga, who shall render a decision as they see fit in case of a disagreement by the two bodies, or confirm the decisions of the two bodies if they are identical.*[43]

The Iroquois Constitution also stipulated a role for women:

> *The women of every clan of the Five Nations shall have a Council Fire ever burning in readiness for a council of the clan. When in their opinion it seems necessary for the interest of the people they shall hold a council and their decisions and recommendations shall be introduced before the Council of the Lords by the War Chief for its consideration.*[44]

Over the years, many people have commented on the similarities between the Great Law of Peace and the United States Constitution. Enough citizens and politicians agreed so that on December 2, 1987, the United States government passed Senate Congressional Resolution 76. Sponsored by Democratic Senator Daniel Inouye of Hawaii, it "Acknowledges the historical debt of the United States to the Iroquois Confederacy and other Indian nations for their demonstration of enlightened, democratic principles of government and their example of a free association of independent Indian nations."[45]

Chapter Seven

GAMES, WEAPONS, AND INTERTRIBAL WARFARE

In the years before the European explorers and settlers arrived, intertribal warfare was a regular occurrence for many Native American groups. Weaponry varied depending on the materials available, and tactics differed by tribe or region. However, methods and styles of fighting were similar, as were rituals related to war and fighting. Games also held an important role in everyday life, as part of the group's spiritual practices, socializing, and preparation for war. The styles of games and materials used to play them also varied between regions and groups.

The Games of Native American Groups

Games were an important part of life for most of the Native Americans. Since the people believed that the games were given to them by their gods, some of the games related to the weather, the harvest, or health. Playing games was a way to improve physical strength, agility, and stamina. Team sports helped the players learn to work together. Watching and playing games were excellent opportunities for socializing. All of these factors were important for daily living, and for conducting warfare. In fact, the Cherokee called stick games "little brother of war." Games varied according to the region and the tribe; some games were played by many groups, while other games were played by only one or a few groups. In most tribes, the males and females played separately.

The Haudenosaunee played Tewaarathon, meaning "they bump hips" which French explorers later called lacrosse. The people believed that their Creator gave them the game, for the purposes of health, strength, and unity. Each player carried a stick with a net at one end. The object of the game was to catch, carry, and pass the

This illustration from 1860 shows the artist's idea of a Choctaw ball game.

ball across the playing field; the winning team scored the most goals. The size of the playing field varied from about 100 yards (91.4 m) to up to 2 miles (3.2 km). Team size also fluctuated from a few players to several hundred.

Snowsnake was another Haudenosaunee game, played in the winter by the male members of the group. The goal was to throw either a 7-foot (2.1 m) stick called a longsnake, or a 3-foot (0.9 m) stick called a mudcat, the longest distance. Throwing the stick for a mile or more was an especially admirable feat.

The Potawatomi of present-day Kansas played a version of lacrosse with two balls made of deer hide. The balls were tied together and thrown into the air.

Shinny, a combination of soccer and street hockey, was played by the Yaquina and many other groups. Teams had varying numbers of players. The length of the field also varied, but was generally not longer than 75 yards (68.6 m). Players used a long wooden stick with a curved hook on one end to push a deer-hide ball toward a goal.

The Game of Silence was allegedly created by Chippewa or Inuit mothers to keep children occupied indoors during the long, cold winters. The children sat in silence. The last one to speak was the winner.

Children also held races, or played counting or throwing games with sticks, beans, and bones. They rolled hoops made from branches. Girls generally had dolls made of cornhusks or other natural materials; some also had miniature houses.

The Purposes of Intertribal Warfare

The motivations for fighting were similar among most Native Americans. Common motivations included such factors as intertribal rivalry or feuding, getting revenge for the killing of one's relatives, or the seizure of captives. It was a custom among the Haudenosaunee, for instance, to adopt such captives into the group to replace deceased members. In addition, some groups looked on war as a sacred activity meant to restore the natural order of a given region, which the invisible spirits supposedly felt was somehow impaired or out of balance.

Sparked by such factors, precontact Native American wars were almost always local, small-scale, and lasted only a short period of time. This generally ensured that one's enemy would survive a conflict intact. "Instances of mass slaughter on the scale of those habitually carried out by the Assyrians, Greeks, Romans, Huns, Ottomans, and Spanish did not occur in aboriginal America," Cherokee historian Tom Holm pointed out. As a result, intertribal conflicts almost never caused "the destruction of entire societies."[46]

Whatever the reasons for these conflicts, almost all precontact Native Americans shared some basic ideals related to warriors and fighting. A young man who went to war was expected to be brave, of course, but also honest and generous. In addition, he should display a high degree of training and discipline. "Indian discipline was founded on individual honor rather than corporal punishment," scholar Armstrong Starkey wrote. A sense of honor, along with common sense, was expected of the commanders:

> *[War] leaders were chosen according to merit based on courage and experience [and] were concerned to save their men's lives and believed that victory did not justify unnecessary sacrifice. There was no disgrace in retreating to await a more favorable occasion for battle ... [Yet] while avoiding unnecessary casualties, the Indians were a martial people, ready to sell their lives dearly in defense of their homes.*[47]

Probably not every warrior was able to live up to these ideals all of the time. However, strong social pressures and expectations made young men strive to achieve them, and they experienced shame or even became social outcasts when they could not.

This artist's depiction from 1841 shows a Comanche chief in traditional dress with several weapons he would have used.

Weapons for Attack

Precontact Native American weapons were made entirely by hand of stone, wood, and in some cases unsmelted metals (such as lumps of copper found in natural settings).

Offensive weapons (those used to attack an enemy) fell into three general groups—those for striking, those for cutting, and those for piercing. The oldest of the striking weapons were simple clubs fashioned of flint or jasper. Some examples had a rounded head, while others had a head shaped like an ax blade. In another version, the head was not attached rigidly to the handle. Rather, it was placed inside a pouch of rawhide, which was attached to a wooden handle. Because the head stayed loose within the material, it imparted a small but damaging whiplash effect when the user swung the weapon. Another kind of club was made of wood or animal bone or both. Such clubs, which were used extensively in the Southwest and the Northwest, could be used either in a traditional overhand stroke to crush a skull or arm, or in an upward stroke to shatter an opponent's jaw.

Cutting weapons most often featured sharpened stone edges. The oldest and simplest version was a chisel-shaped blade made from a thin piece of jasper, flint, chert, or agate. When attached to a handle fashioned of wood, bone, or horn, the blade became a knife.

The most common piercing weapon was the spear. It could be used in hand-to-hand combat, in which case the user jabbed it overhand at an opponent. More often however, the spear, or a shorter pointed shaft, was thrown, hurled, or propelled from a spot some distance from the target. Only rarely did Native Americans throw such spears or shafts using just the hand. Most often they used a second launching device, the earliest common example being the atlatl. Another device, used by the Miwok and Pomo in California, among others, consisted of a rawhide sling. The Seminoles, Choctaw, and Cherokee in the Southeast developed a blow tube; it worked by placing a short pointed shaft, or dart, in a hollow piece of sugarcane and forcefully blowing it out of the tube.

Another propulsion system—the bow—made the arrow the most widely distributed Native American piercing weapon after about AD 500–700. Virtually every group in North America eventually adopted the bow and arrow. The most prevalent kind of bow was the simple or self bow, made of a single piece of a bendable variety of wood, such as hickory, ash, or black locust. Another type of bow, the reinforced bow, was so named because the wood was backed by a strip of animal sinew to give it more flexibility and power. Reinforced bows were generally made of cedar, juniper, ash, or wild plum, though other kinds of wood were also used.

The arrows had heads fashioned from flint and other types of stone, as well as horn, bone, wood, seashell, and unprocessed copper. An arrowhead was most often triangular in shape. The warrior

Arrowheads were often made of flint or other types of stone, as well as materials such as bone, wood, horn, and seashell.

joined it to the shaft by inserting it in a notch in the wood and lashing it tight with strips of sinew. It was also important that the shafts be straight and fitted with feathers to ensure balanced, accurate flight after leaving the bow. "A crooked arrow or one with improperly placed guide feathers proved worthless," Carlson pointed out. With great care, he said, the arrow makers

> *cut the shafts to the desired length and shape, tied them in a bunch, and to season them hung them near a fire for about ten days. Then, in a tedious process [they] straightened the shafts. Over a period of several days, they used their teeth, grease, fire, and a special arrow straightener—a bone or horn with a hole slightly larger than the shaft through which they passed the arrow back and forth—to make the arrow perfectly round ... Next, they polished and painted the shaft. Finally, they attached the feathers—owl, turkey, or buzzard feathers preferred—with glue and fixed the point.*[48]

Weapons for Defense

Precontact Native Americans also employed various defensive military devices and methods. Many used body armor, composed of wood, bone, ivory, and animal hides. An excellent example of wooden Native American armor is a surviving cuirass (chest protector) of the Tlingit people, who dwelled in the

Northwest Coast region. The front section contains ten vertical wooden slats bound together with strips of animal sinew and rawhide. Attached to the end slats are sections made of lightweight, somewhat flexible wooden rods, also placed vertically. Wide rawhide strips attached to the top of the front section of the armor ran back over the wearer's shoulders and connected to the back section, which was made of slats like the front. The Huron and some other Haudenosaunee groups of the Northeast also wore elaborate armor composed of wooden rods and slats.

In addition, the Tlingit and some other Native American groups used protective helmets. They made these from either bundles of small wooden rods or a single, carved piece of wood. Some Tlingit helmets even had movable visors.

Another common kind of Native American armor was crafted from layers of animal hides. Some northwestern groups used it, as did the Shoshone, Pawnee, and several other Great Plains groups, the Navajo in the Southwest, and the Mohawk in New York. Such armor generally featured two or more layers of hide stitched together with rawhide strips. Elk hide was widely used, although hides from moose, bison, and other large mammals were also employed in various areas. Hide armor was also used to protect the horses of the Shoshone and some other Great Plains peoples.

Another kind of defensive device used widely by the Native Americans was a circular shield made of tree bark, wood, and dried animal hides. The Comanche, in the southern Great Plains, carried a version fashioned from two pieces of rawhide laced together around a wooden hoop. The space in the middle was stuffed with feathers, grass, horse hair, or some other bendable material to help slow the momentum of a club or arrow. Most such shields were about three feet (1 m) in diameter and featured a neck strap that allowed a warrior to carry his shield on his side, shoulder, or back. Many Native Americans felt that their shields could be made to possess supernatural properties that increased the owners' level of protection. To that end, they painted on the shields designs meant to invoke the powers of various spirits or animal or sky gods.

A certain amount of military protection was also gained by various kinds of defense structures used by precontact Native Americans, particularly those who lived in the Southwest and the Eastern Woodlands. Some of these defenses were quite large and elaborate, notably the wooden stockades erected by the Haudenosaunee around their villages. Sometimes earthen embankments (or raised areas of dirt) were built outside the stockade for extra protection. Some northeastern Native Americans also created moatlike ditches to help keep attackers from entering the village.

In the Southwest, fortifications seem to have been designed more to protect a central ceremonial center and members

This photograph shows the great amount of detail that can be seen in traditional Native American dress.

Settlers Adopt Native American Armor

Although on occasion some Native American groups did copy various elements of the armor they saw worn by early European explorers, the process often worked the other way around. That is, a number of early settlers who lacked armor adopted already existing Native American versions. A memorable example is the case of Captain John Smith, the renowned co-founder of the English colony of Jamestown, in Virginia. In 1608 he found himself under attack by a local group. A different group, which had established friendship with Smith and the other settlers, helped him and his men put on Native American-made wooden armor. This armor was so effective that, in the words of one of the colonists, it "securely beat back the savages from off the plain without [our receiving] any hurt."[1]

1. Quoted in Colin F. Taylor, *Native American Weapons*. Norman, OK: University of Oklahoma Press, 2001, p. 123.

of an elite social class. "Many of the principal towns erected by the southeastern tribes were religious sanctuaries as well as … administrative centers," scholar Norman Bancroft-Hunt explained.

> *The descriptions we have suggest these towns were protected by palisades [fences], ditches, and earth embankments, and sometimes even by moats, with the house of the chief, the temples of the priests, and the dwellings of other dignitaries raised on earthen mounds protected by secondary palisades or walls. By far the larger part of the population lived outside these massive fortifications, and the only permanent occupancy was by an exclusive class of civil, military, and religious leaders, who were guarded by warrior societies whose specific function was to protect the nobility and priests.*[49]

Strategies, Tactics, and Rituals

All across North America, Native Americans developed similar modes of military offense and defense. The actual strategies and tactics they used fell into four broad forms or categories, with numerous minor variations from place to place. In the open Great Plains and other non-forested areas, it was common for opposing warriors to line up opposite each other and fire atlatls or arrows back and forth. Because shields were used by both sides, casualties were generally very light, and after a while the opposing forces would go home, feeling satisfied that they had vented their anger.

A second, more lethal kind of combat involved a war chief leading his men in a charge that led to hand-to-hand combat with clubs or knives. The outcome was generally brief and bloody. The third general kind of combat was common in both the Eastern Woodlands and the mountainous areas of the Southwest. The warriors generally spread out and used trees, rocks, and other forms of cover. The fourth major tactical approach, one practiced all across the continent, was to launch raids on enemy villages or camps. Such raids most often took place before dawn so that the attackers could take advantage of the darkness and the fact that most of the enemy were sleeping. Typically, the raiders swept into the village, killed a number of victims swiftly, and then slipped away before the survivors could organize a proper defense.

The warriors who achieved a successful raid or other military victory acquired much prestige in their community. However, sometimes such attacks failed. This was a problem for the attackers because their people might view them as cowards. To avoid such an outcome, many Native American groups developed special war rituals that substituted for actual combat. When Tlingit raiders were unable to penetrate an enemy village, for example, they put on a loud, spirited display of intimidation instead. The warriors climbed into canoes, rowed to a point within shouting distance of the village, verbally taunted the villagers, and called on various gods and spirits to curse them. To save face, the villagers then produced their own shaman, who aimed a similar barrage of curses and threats at the raiders. Finally, the intruders departed, leaving behind few or no casualties on either side.

Similar mock battle rituals developed among numerous other Native American groups. This was one of the reasons that their wars rarely, if ever, wiped out entire towns or peoples. That would change, however, when Native Americans started fighting against the new settlers who had come to claim their lands.

Epilogue

THE EUROPEAN ONSLAUGHT

Once news of Columbus's discovery reached Europe, the Spanish conquistadors started the demise of the Native Americans. Other nations quickly followed. According to O'Brien,

> *Beginning with Columbus and his colony on the island of Hispaniola, the Spanish developed an ideological weapon against Indians that denied them their inherent humanity. Spanish views of Indians as either kind and gentle or mean and aggressive, noble or ignoble, described Native Americans in terms of what they were not: they were not "civilized" and not Christian. Beginning with Columbus's letters, printing presses spread this initial Spanish view of Indians throughout Europe, and the view of Indians as uncivilized, irrational, and often violent became entrenched in European minds. Such imagery was in turn used by all European colonizers to justify taking Indian lands and enslaving Indian people.*[50]

In short, the European onslaught—consisting of theft of Native American lands, infection of the peoples with deadly diseases, the forcible removal of whole communities onto remote reservations, and the forcible herding of those who resisted—decimated traditional Native American civilization. Even though, a few hundred years later, the United States government began making some reparations, the widespread damage could not be undone.

Debilitating Diseases

Researchers believe that there were between 8 to 30 million Native Americans living in precontact North America,

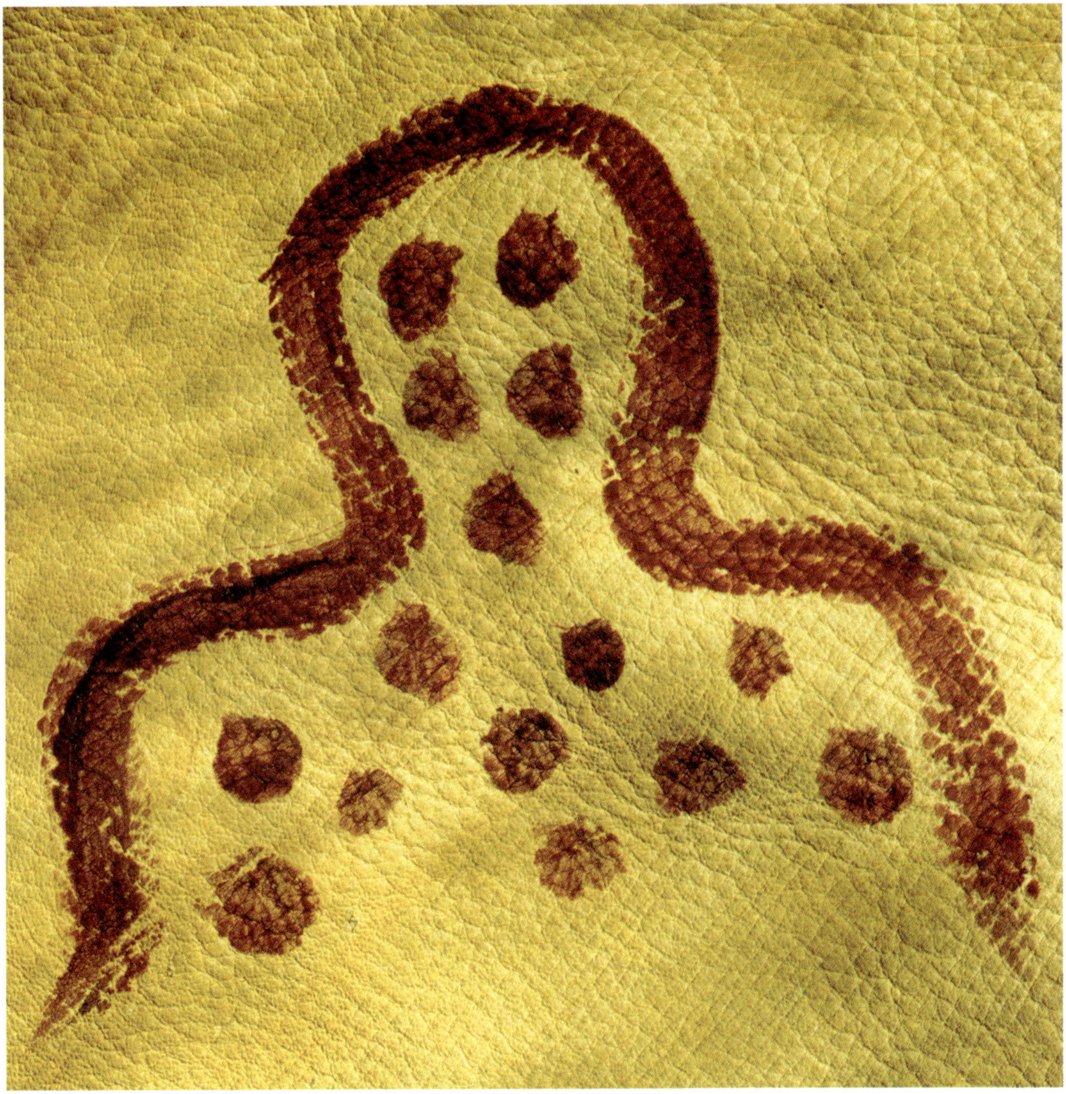

This cave painting depicts a man suffering from smallpox.

and that the Native Americans were, as a whole, healthier and had fewer diseases and disease-related deaths than did their European counterparts.[51]

The Europeans brought "bubonic plague, chicken pox … cholera, diphtheria, influenza, measles, scarlet fever, smallpox, typhus, tuberculosis, and whooping cough."[52] Journals and other written texts from the period indicate that smallpox was the deadliest of the diseases. Because of lack of previous exposure, the Native Americans had no natural immunity—and no way to treat the diseases. Some accounts estimate that up to 90 percent of the Native American population died from these highly contagious diseases.

In 1585, English explorer Thomas Harriot described the aftermath of contact between Europeans and Native Americans in a North Carolina village:

> *Within a few days after our departure from every such [Indian] town, the people began to die very fast, and many in short spade; in some towns about twenty, in some forty, in some sixty, & in one six score [6 x 20 = 120], which in truth was very many in respect of their numbers. . . . The disease was also so strange that they neither know what it was nor how to cure it.*[53]

The tragic fate of the Massachuset illustrates the fate of many of the groups. The earliest European explorers brought germs with them, which they quickly, although unknowingly, spread. Between 1614 and 1617, epidemics wiped out three-quarters of the Massachuset, many of whom had not even seen an explorer or settler. By the time the Pilgrims landed at Plymouth in 1620, most of the Native American villages had already been abandoned. By 1640, the group had almost completely been wiped out. The scenario repeated itself all over the continent as the Europeans and Native Americans made increased contact.

Logistical Advantages

When European settlers arrived in North America, they brought not just devastating diseases, but also advanced weapons, such as guns and cannons. Settlers would sometimes sell these weapons to certain groups to encourage them to fight one another, which made them less likely to fight the settlers as they encroached on their lands.

Settlers also tried to gain favor with Native American groups by promising them things that they never intended to give them. For example, during the American Revolution, both the British and the Americans tried to bring Native American groups to their side by promising them land. When the war ended, however, the victorious Americans did not honor those promises. Instead, the new U.S. government was working to take over more Native American lands to expand the young country. They planned to do this by removing Native Americans from their homelands and relocating them to places that were often far from any environment they were familiar with.

Removal and Reservations

The United States Constitution, written in 1787, did not consider Native Americans to be citizens, and the new U.S. government put the Committee on Indian Affairs, led by Benjamin Franklin, under the Department of War. A few years later, President Thomas Jefferson supported removal,

This photograph shows the aftermath of the Wounded Knee Massacre in 1890.

but he did not act on it. Meanwhile, increasing numbers of soldiers, settlers, guns, and horses, plus expanding networks of railroads and advanced communications, including the telegraph, all worked against the Native Americans, who were increasingly on the defensive. Even when the groups had given up fighting, the intruding settlers did not even attempt to live in peaceful harmony.

On May 28, 1830, President Andrew Jackson signed the Indian Removal act. This inhumane policy authorized the removal of Native Americans from their ancestral lands and relocating them to "Indian Country," remote, mostly unproductive reservations west of the Mississippi.

When the Cherokee refused to move from their Georgia home, President Martin Van Buren sent 7,000 troops against them. The soldiers dragged the Cherokee from their houses and drove them in a forced march that was later referred to as The Trail of Tears. Private John G. Burnett, one of the soldiers assigned to the action, wrote,

> *On the morning of November the 17th we encountered a terrific*

sleet and snow storm with freezing temperatures and from that day on until we reached the end of the fateful journey on March the 26th 1839, the sufferings of the Cherokees were awful. The trail of the exiles was a trail of death. They had to sleep in the wagons and on the ground without fire. And I have known as many as twenty-two of them to die in one night of pneumonia due to ill treatment, cold, and exposure.[54]

In all, more than 4,000 Cherokee died on the Trail of Tears. Meanwhile, back in Georgia, gangs of settlers looted the empty Cherokee houses and burned them to the ground.

To the Edge of Extinction and Back Again

Many of the displaced Native Americans believed that their bravery, continued fighting, and faith in help from their gods and spirits would eventually bring them to victory. Sadly, this was not the case, and the wars and removals continued. The government still tried to destroy Native American cultures, languages, religions, and lifestyles in the name of making them into their idea of real Americans.

The last of the Indian Wars—the general name sometimes given to the conflicts between Native Americans and U.S. settlers—took place on December 29, 1890 at Wounded Knee Creek in South Dakota. The U.S. troops killed about 300 Sioux, including women and children, and 25 soldiers died. After that, the remaining Native Americans lived mostly on the reservations, in poverty, and without rights as citizens of the United States. Many times, the children were sent away to boarding schools.

In the 20th century, government policies began to change in favor of the Native Americans, due to increased activism by many American Indian individuals and nations. In 1934, Congress passed the Indian Reorganization Act (IRA, also known as the Wheeler-Howard Act). The act allowed groups to organize their own governments, encouraged economic development, and promoted civil and cultural rights. The groups that voted in favor of the act wrote their own constitutions, based on the U. S. Constitution, and began to govern themselves as sovereign nations within the U. S. government. In 2012, the federal government paid out a total of $3.4 million to Native Americans as settlement of a lawsuit related to land ownership.

The Bureau of Indian Affairs (BIA), created in 1824, evolved from the earlier Committee on Indian Affairs. The BIA provides for, among other things, "disaster relief, Indian child welfare, tribal government,"[55] and land management.

According to the 2014 Census, there are about 5.4 million Native Americans and Alaska Natives in the United States. Fifteen states have

Many groups hold powwows to celebrate their heritage. Most powwows are open to the public.

more than 100,000 American Indian or Alaska Native residents, or a mixture of both groups. There are 326 federally recognized Native American reservations and 566 federally recognized Native American groups. (A federally recognized group has a legal relationship with the U. S. government.) Native Americans still face difficulties related to housing, employment, health, education, and other issues.

In 2016, national attention was drawn to Native American issues through the controversy surrounding the Dakota Access Pipeline, a major oil pipeline project. The proposed path of the pipeline was meant to cut through lands that are sacred to the Standing Rock Sioux Tribe, as well as areas that could have affected the Sioux people's water supply. Large numbers of protestors traveled to stand alongside the Sioux people and against the pipeline's continued construction. In December 2016, the Department of the Army announced that the pipeline would not be drilled in these lands as originally planned, which was a major victory for the Sioux people. Many are concerned, though, that this plan could change in the future with the change in presidential leadership in the United States.

Despite the struggles faced by Native American groups in modern times, a rising interest in the languages and cultures gives hope that conditions will continue to improve and that greater respect will be given to Native Americans across the United States. According to activist Buffy Sainte-Marie, "Indians Exist. We are alive and real. We have fun, friends, families, and a whole lot to contribute to the rest of the world through our reality."[56]

Notes

Introduction: A Rich and Complex History

1. Edmund J. Ladd, "Archaeology and Indians," in Frederick E. Hoxie, *Encyclopedia of North American Indians*. Boston, MA: Houghton Mifflin, 1996, p. 33.
2. Quoted in Ladd, "Archaeology and Indians," p. 34.
3. Brian M. Fagan, *Ancient North America*. New York, NY: Thames and Hudson, 2005, p. 67.
4. Fagan, *Ancient North America*, p. 68.

Chapter One: Origin Theories

5. Quoted in Howard Zinn, "History is a Weapon: A People's History of the United States." www.historyisaweapon.com/defcon1/zinncol1.html.
6. Indigenous Peoples' Literature, "Chelan Creation Myth: Creation of the First Indians," Indians.org. www.indians.org/welker/firstind.htm.
7. 2 Kings 17:6 (New King James Version).
8. Quoted in *NOVA*, "Where Are the Ten Lost Tribes?," PBS. www.pbs.org/wgbh/nova/israel/losttribes2.html.
9. Quoted in E. James Dixon, *Quest for the Origins of the First Americans*. Albuquerque, NM: University of New Mexico Press, 1993, p. 3.
10. Quoted in Brian M. Fagan, *The Great Journey: The Peopling of Ancient America*. Miami, FL: University Press of Florida, 2003, p. 34.
11. Philip Kopper, *The Smithsonian Book of North American Indians*. New York, NY: Harry N. Abrams, 1986, p. 31.
12. Fagan, *Great Journey*, pp. 133–134.

Chapter Two: The Earliest North Americans

13. Fagan, *Ancient North America*, p. 91.
14. Fagan, *Ancient North America*, p. 89.
15. Quoted in Kopper, *Smithsonian Book of North American Indians*, p. 40.
16. Quoted in Space Daily, "New Clovis-Age Comet Impact Theory," May 23, 2007. www.spacedaily.com/reports/New_Clovis_Age_Comet_Impact_Theory_999.html.
17. Arrell M. Gibson, *The American Indian: Prehistory to the Present*. Lexington, MA: D.C. Heath, 1980, p. 21.

Chapter Three: Native Americans of the West

18. Quoted in Kopper, *Smithsonian Book of North American Indians*, p. 201.

19. Kopper, *Smithsonian Book of North American Indians*, p. 217.
20. Kopper, *Smithsonian Book of North American Indians*, p. 191.
21. Quoted in Kopper, *Smithsonian Book of North American Indians*, p. 193.
22. Carl Waldman, *Atlas of the North American Indian*. New York, NY: Facts On File, 1985, p. 39.
23. Waldman, *Atlas of the North American Indian*, p. 18.
24. Gibson, *The American Indian*, p. 75.

Chapter Four: Native Americans of the Great Plains

25. Greg O'Brien. *The Timeline of Native Americans*. San Diego, CA: Thunder Bay Press, 2008, p. 20.
26. Fagan, *Ancient North America*, pp. 131–132.
27. "Bow and Arrow," Indians.org. www.indians.org/articles/bow-and-arrows.html.
28. Ken Deaver and Sherri Deaver, Encyclopedia of the Great Plains. plainshumanities.unl.edu/encyclopedia/doc/egp.arc.048.
29. Quoted in Fagan, *Ancient North America*, p. 138.
30. Paul H. Carlson, *The Plains Indians*. College Station, TX: Texas A&M University Press, 1998, p. 39.
31. Jeffrey E. Davis, *Hand Talk: Sign Language Among American Indian Nations*. Cambridge, UK: Cambridge University Press, 2016. www.cambridge.org/catalogue/catalogue.asp?isbn=9780521870108.

Chapter Five: Early Native Americans of the Southeast

32. Thomas Jefferson, "*Notes on the State of Virginia*, chap. 11," American Studies at the University of Virginia. xroads.virginia.edu/~hyper/JEFFERSON/ch11.html.
33. James A. Brown, "Mound Builders," in Hoxie, *Encyclopedia of North American Indians*, p. 398.
34. O'Brien, *Timeline of Native Americans*, p. 29.
35. Quoted in Kopper, *Smithsonian Book of North American Indians*, pp. 164–165.
36. Quoted in Timothy R. Pauketat, "Cahokia: A Pre-Columbian American City," History Now: The Journal of the Gilder Leheman Institute. www.gilderlehrman.org/history-by-era/american-indians/essays/cahokia-pre-columbian-american-city.

Chapter Six: Native Americans of the Northeastern Woodlands

37. Quoted in Hoxie, *Encyclopedia of North American Indians*, pp. 680–681.
38. Kopper, *Smithsonian Book of North American Indians*, p. 140.
39. Internet Modern History Sourcebook, "The Constitution of the Iroquois Confederacy." www.fordham.edu/halsall/mod/iroquois.html.
40. Quoted in "Haudenosaunee Guide for Educators," National Musuem

of the American Indian. nmai.si.edu/sites/1/files/pdf/education/HaudenosauneeGuide-2016.pdf.
41. O'Brien, *Timeline of Native Americans*, p. 84.
42. Fagan, *Ancient North America*, p. 505.
43. Internet Modern History Sourcebook, "The Constitution of the Iroquois Confederacy."
44. Quoted in "Pre-Columbian to the New Millennium," U.S. History. www.ushistory.org/us/1d.asp.
45. Quoted in U.S. Congress, "S.Con.Res.76 - A concurrent resolution to acknowledge the contribution of the Iroquois Confederacy of Nations to the Development of the United States Constitution and to reaffirm the continuing government-to-government relationship between Indian tribes and the United States established in the Constitution," Congress.gov. 1987–1988. www.congress.gov/bill/100th-congress/senate-concurrent-resolution/76.

Chapter Seven: Games, Weapons, and Intertribal Warfare

46. Tom Holm, "Warriors and Warfare," in Hoxie, *Encyclopedia of North American Indians*, p. 666.
47. Armstrong Starkey, *European and Native American Warfare, 1675–1815*. Norman, OK: University of Oklahoma Press, 1998, pp. 21–22.
48. Carlson, *The Plains Indians*, p. 62.
49. Norman Bancroft-Hunt, *Warriors: Warfare and the Native American Indian*. London, UK: Salamander, 1995, pp. 22–23.

Epilogue: The European Onslaught

50. O'Brien, *Timeline of Native Americans*, pp. 43-44.
51. Neil Schlager and Josh Lauer, eds., "The Impact of European Diseases on Native Americans." *Science and Its Times*. Vol. 3. Detroit, MI: Gale, 2001.
52. Quoted in Ojibwa, "American Indians and European Diseases," Native American Netroots. nativeamericannetroots.net/diary/325.
53. Quoted in John Kincheloe III, "American Indians at European contact," NCPedia. ncpedia.org/history/early/contact.
54. Quoted in Cherokees of California, "Cherokee Removal-The Trail Where They Cried nu na hi du na tlo hi lu i." www.powersource.com/cocinc/history/trail.htm.
55. Bureau of Indian Affairs (BIA), "Who We Are." www.bia.gov/WhoWeAre/BIA.
56. Quoted in Buffy Sainte-Marie, "Foreword," Children of Native America Today. cradleboard.org/cnat/index.html.

For More Information

Books

Ciovacco, Justine. *Discovering Native North American Cultures*. New York, NY: Britannica Educational Publishing, 2015.
Ciovacco gives readers an overview of the many distinct Native American cultural groups that can be found in North America.

Dunbar-Ortiz, Roxanne. *An Indigenous Peoples' History of the United States*. Boston MA: Beacon Press, 2014.
This book describes the history of the early United States told from the perspective of indigenous peoples.

Levy, Janey. *Native Peoples of the Northwest Coast*. New York, NY: Gareth Stevens Publishing, 2016.
Levy presents a brief history of the Native Americans who lived in modern-day Alaska, Oregon, Washington, northern California, and British Columbia.

Lopenzia, Drew. *Through an Indian's Looking Glass: A Cultural Biography of William Apess, Pequot*. Amherst, MA: University of Massachusetts Press, Reprint Edition, 2017.
This is a biography of William Apess (1789-1839), who was a Pequot Indian, a Methodist preacher, and a writer.

Martinez, Donna and Jennifer Williams Bordeaux, eds. *50 Events That Shaped American Indian History: An Encyclopedia of the American Mosaic* [2 volumes], Santa Barbara, CA: Greenwood, 2017.
Native American history scholars and Native American peoples share their perspectives on important historical events in these two volumes.

Websites

America's Stone Age Explorers (www.pbs.org/wgbh/nova/stoneage)
This website is related to the *NOVA* series on early Americans, with several links to related articles.

Bering Land Bridge: National Preserve Alaska (www.nps.gov/bela/learn/historyculture/index.htm)
Information about this important national park is provided, as well as historical information about migration theories, climate change, and the history and culture of the area.

"The Clovis Point and the Discovery of America's First Culture" (www.smithsonianmag.com/history/the-clovis-point-and-the-discovery-of-americas-first-culture-3825828/)
This article provides a detailed account of the discovery of the Clovis point and the history of the related culture.

Native American Cultures (www.history.com/topics/native-american-history/native-american-cultures)
This History Channel site includes articles, videos, pictures, and speeches related to the history of Native Americans.

National Park Service: Indian Mounds of Mississippi (www.nps.gov/nr/travel/mounds/builders.htm)
This site provides information about the mound builders of the Mississippian period. It also includes relevant maps and photographs.

Index

A

Acosta, José de, 17–19
Adena culture, 6, 57, 59, 62
agriculture
  of Algonquians, 67
  development of, 31
  on the Great Plains, 6, 44, 47
  of Mississipian culture, 62
  of Pueblo peoples, 41
  slash and burn, 70
  of Southwestern tribes, 41
Aikens, Melvin, 39
Alabama, 54–55
Alaska, 18–20, 25, 32–33, 90–91
Algonquians, 65–68, 74
American Antiquarian Society, 18
American Indians. *See* Native Americans
Ancestral Puebloans, 7, 41–42, 64
ancestral spirits, 52
ancient civilizations
  dating of, 22
  study of, 8–11
  See also precontact era
animal species
  of Great Plains, 45, 47, 49–53
  migration of, 18–21
  See also specific species
Apache, 32–33, 41, 43, 49
Arapaho, 49
archaeologists
  Native Americans opinion of, 9
  study of precontact cultures by, 8–11
Archaeology of the United States (Haven), 18
Archaic cultures
  dating of, 22–23
  development of agriculture by, 30–31
  hunting methods, 23–24
  regional diversification of, 29
  spear points of, 24, 26
  See also specific tribes
Arikaras, 48
armor, 27, 81–82, 84
arrows, 6, 27, 46–47, 50–51, 72, 80–82, 84
artifacts
  of Hopewell culture, 59–60
  Makah, 35–36
  microblades, 20
  return of, 10
  Stone Age, 20
Asian ancestry, 20
Assiniboin, 49
Atlantis, 17
atlatl, 23–24, 27, 46, 80, 84
Aztecs, 23–24, 61

B

Bancroft-Hunt, Norman, 84
baskets, Pomo, 38
battlefields
  honor on, 78
  tactics on, 84–85
beans, 30–31, 39–40, 43, 47, 62, 67, 78
Bering Land Bridge, 18–19
Bering Strait,19
Bering, Vitus, 18
Beringia, 19, 20, 22
Besant point, 46
Bible, 16
bison
  of Great Plains, 44–45
  Horse and Bison Culture, 50, 52–53
  hunting of, 28, 30, 45–47, 49–50, 53
  Paleo-Indians and, 27–28
bison corrals, 45
bison jump, 47
Blackfeet, 48
blades, 15, 20, 24, 26, 80
blow tubes, 80
boats, 15, 21, 24, 36
Book of Mormon, The, 17
bow and arrow, 6, 46–47, 50, 80
Bradley, Bruce, 25
Brown, James A., 56
Bureau of American Ethnology, 57
Bureau of Indian Affairs, 90
burial mounds, 56, 59
  See also Mound Builders
burial sites, 9, 54–55

C

Caddo, 47
Cahokia complex, 54, 62–64
California, 32–33, 38–40, 80
Canada, 19, 22, 25, 32, 44, 65–66
candlefish, 35
Carlson, Paul H., 49, 81
Carthaginians, 15–16
Catlin, George, 51
cave painting, 87
Cayugas, 66, 72–73, 75
Cayuse, 37
Central America, 6, 61
ceramics, 40
Chatters, James, 10
Chelan, 14, 16
Cherokee, 55, 75, 78, 80, 89–90
Cheyenne, 49

Chickasaw, 55
chiefdoms, 54–55, 62–63
Chillicothe, 59–60
Chilula, 39
Chinook, 33–34
Choctaw, 55, 77, 80
Christians, 16, 86
clan, 36, 43, 71–73, 75
Clovis culture
camps, 25–26
classification of, 22
hunting methods, 23–24
transition to Folsom culture, 23, 26, 29
Clovis point, 22–24, 26, 28
collaborative research, 11
Columbia, 37
Columbia River, 10, 39
Columbus, Christopher
description of natives by, 12, 15
discovery of Americas by, 7, 12
Comanche, 49, 51, 79, 82
combat, 80, 85
See also war
comet, 29
Composite Plains Culture, 52
corn, 31, 41, 44, 67
crafts, 39–40, 60
creation myths, 14–15
Cree, 49
Creek, 55
crops, 8, 31, 42–44, 47, 50, 54, 62–63, 70
See also agriculture
Crow, 49
cultural exchange, 33
culture gap, 9
Cusabo, 55
Custer, Jay F., 26

D
De Soto, Hernando, 12, 27
diet, 10, 39, 47, 55, 67
See also agriculture
diseases, 8, 10, 86–88
ditches, 41, 82, 84
DNA evidence, on Asian ancestry, 20
dogs, 44, 49, 52
Dyuktai Cave site, 20

E
earth lodges, 48
environmental changes, 29
epidemics, 88
Erlandson, Jon M., 29
Europeans
conquest by, 8, 86
technological advancements by, 8
weapons of, 8, 88
extinction
of Massachuset group, 88
of Native American groups, 53, 90
of Stone Age mammals, 28
extraterrestrial impact theory, 29

F
Fagan, Brian M.
on bison hunting, 45–46
on collaborative research, 11
on food sources, 25
on Iroquois Confederacy, 73
on mammoths, 24–25
on migration of Native American ancestors, 21
on reburial, 10
farming. *See* agriculture
fishing methods, 35, 39
Folsom culture
classification of, 23
Clovis culture versus, 26
transition from Clovis culture to, 23, 26, 29
weaponry of, 26, 28
Folsom point, 26, 28
food sources, 25, 30, 32, 39, 48, 67
fortifications, 82, 84
Four Corners area, 41
Fremont culture, 37
Frison, George, 24

G
Gibson, Arrell M., 29, 41, 43
gift-giving, 38, 49
gravesites, 10
Great Basin, 32, 36–37, 39
Great Chief (Great Spirit), 14, 16
Great Plains
animals of, 45
eastern plains, 47
groups of the, 23, 32, 44
territory of, 44
Great Serpent Mound, 59

H
Haida, 33–34
Harriot, Thomas, 88
hatchets, 49
Haudenosaunee
dwellings of, 69–71
games of, 76–77
groups of the, 65–66
matrilineal system, 71–72
political system, 72–73
role of women, 71
warfare customs, 78, 82
Havasupai, 41
Haven, Samuel, 18
Hiawatha, 72–73
Holm, Tom, 78
Hopewell culture, 6, 59–62
Hopi, 9, 33, 41, 43
Horse and Bison Culture, 50, 52–53
horses
impact of, 49–50, 52
introduction of, 7, 45, 49
houses
Algonquian, 68–69
Clovis, 25–26
earth, 48
Haudenosaunee, 69–71
longhouses, 35, 69–72
Mississipian, 54
of Northwest Coast groups, 35–36
pit, 37, 41
of Plains Woodland Native Americans, 48

pueblos, 41–43
tepees, 48, 50
wigwams, 68
hunter-gatherers, 20, 22, 25, 32, 37, 40
hunting methods
of Clovis peoples, 23–24
of Great Basin Indians, 37
horses and, 52
of Northwest Coast tribes, 33, 35
of Plains Indians, 45–47
Hurons, 65, 82

I
Ice Age mammals
extinction of, 28
mammoths, 19, 23–24, 28, 30
Idaho, 32
Indian Removal Act, 89
Indian Wars, 8, 90
intertribal warfare
reasons for, 78
weapons used in, 80–82, 84
Iroquois. *See* Haudenosaunee
Iroquois Confederacy, 7, 66, 72, 74–75
Iroquois constitution, 75
Israel, 16, 57

J
Jefferson, Thomas, 55–56
Jesuit missionaries, 17

K
Kato, 39
Kennett, Douglas J., 29
Kennewick Man, 10–11
Klamath, 37
Kopper, Philip
on Iroquois, 70
on migration, 20
on potlatches, 36
Kroeber, Alfred L., 38

L
Ladd, Edmund J., 9
Lamanites, 17
land bridge, 8, 18–19
languages
of Algonquians, 65, 67
diversification of, 31
of Plains Indians, 53
lodges
Clovis, 25–26
earth, 48
See also houses
longhouses, 35, 69–72
Lumnius, Joannes, 16

M
maize, 30–31, 37, 40, 47
Makah, 33, 35–36
mammoths
extinction of, 28
hunting of, 23–24
Mandan, 44, 47–48, 50
Martin, Paul, 28
Mashantucket Pequot Museum, 9
Mashantucket Pequots, 9
Massachusetts, 65, 67
matrilineal groups, 54, 71–72
McCulloh, James, 57
megafauna, 28
Mesoamerican Native Americans, 61
meteor, 29
Micmac, 65
microblades, 20
migration
across Beringia, 18–21
of animals, 23, 44
of Apache, 32, 41, 49
of Archaic peoples, 23, 31
from Asia, 8
to California, 39
in creation myths, 14–15
dating of, 8
European beliefs of, 15–18
of Folsom peoples, 29
of Great Basin peoples, 37
to the Great Plains, 44
of Haudenosaunee, 65
of Mesoamericans, 61
Solutrean hypothesis of, 21
of Tuscarora, 72
missionaries, 13, 17
Mississippian culture, 54, 61–62
Miwok, 39, 80
Mogollon peoples, 40
Mohawk, 65–66, 72–73, 75, 82
Mojave, 41
Montezinos, Antonio, 17
Mormons, 17
Mound Builders
Adena culture, 57, 59
decline of, 63–64
earliest, 61
Hopewell culture, 59
Poverty Point, 57–59
mystery surrounding, 56–57
Temple, 62

N
Narragansett, 65, 67–68
Natchez, 55, 64
Native Americans
decimation of, 86–92
impact of horses on, 49–50, 52
origins of, 18–21
relocation of, 88–90
study of ancient, 9–11
warfare among, 78
Native American Grave Protection and Repatriation Act (NAGPRA), 10–11
Natural and Moral History of the Indians (Acosta), 17
Nauset, 67–68
Nephites, 17
New England, 65, 67
Newark, Ohio, 60
Nez Perce, 16
nomadic hunters, 50
See also hunting methods
Nootka, 33
Northwest Coast peoples, 32–33, 36, 82
Notes on the State of Virginia (Jefferson), 55

O
Ohio Valley, 54
Oneidas, 66, 72–73, 75
Onondagas, 66, 69, 72–73, 75
Oraibi pueblo, 43
Oregon, 32
overkill hypothesis, 28
Oviedo y Valdes, Gonzalo Fernandez de, 17
Ozette, Washington, 33, 35–36

P
Paiute, 36
Paleo-Indians
  Clovis hunters, 22–26, 29
  Folsom peoples, 23, 26, 28–29
Pawauog, 68
Pawnee, 44, 47, 50, 82
Peacemaker, 72
Phoenicians, 15–16
Pilgrims, 67, 88
Pit houses, 37, 41
Plains Native Americans
  hunting methods of, 45–47, 53
  impact of horses on, 49–50, 52
  lodging of, 48
  sign language of, 53
Plains Woodland Native Americans, 47
Political systems
  of Algonquians, 67–68
  of Haudenosaunee, 72–73
  matrilineal clans, 54, 71–72
  of Mississipian culture, 55
Pomo, 38–39, 80
Pomo baskets, 38
potlatches, 34, 36
pottery making, 40–41, 60
Poverty Point, 57–59
psychotropic plants, 43
Pueblo peoples, 43
pueblo houses, 41–43
pumpkins, 31, 43

R
rabbit hunts, 37
raids, 49, 52, 85
reburials, of artifacts, 10
religions
  of Algonquians, 68
  destruction of, 90
  similarities among, 43
religious rituals
  of Plains Native Americans, 52–53
  of Pueblo peoples, 41–43
relocation policy, 88–90
reservations, 9, 86, 88–91
rituals
  burial, 61
  religious, 41–43, 52–53
  war, 76, 84–85
Ruby corral, 45–46

S
sachems, 67
sacrifice, 43, 78
Salish, 33–34
Saucier, Roger, 58
Seminole, 55, 80
Seneca, 65–66, 72–73, 75
shamanism, 43, 68, 85
shields, 51, 82, 84
Shoshone, 36, 49, 82
Siberia, 18–20, 22, 25
sign language, 53
Sioux, 49, 83, 90–92
slash and burn agriculture, 70
smallpox, 8, 87
Smith, Bruce D., 62
Smith, John, 84
Solutrean hypothesis, 25
Southeastern groups, 54–55, 59, 84
  See also Mound Builders
Southwestern groups, 9, 32, 40–41, 49
spears, 12, 23, 39, 45–46, 80
Speth, John, 53
spirits, 43, 52, 68, 78, 82, 85, 90
squash, 30–31, 40, 47, 67
Stanford, Dennis, 25
Starkey, Armstrong, 78
Stockades, 70
Stone Age culture, 20, 23, 25, 28
stone blades, 20, 69, 82
stone tools and weapons
  of Clovis peoples, 22–24, 26, 28
  of Folsom peoples, 26, 28
  offensive weapons, 81–82
  striking, 80
supernatural world, 16, 34, 43, 52, 68, 82

T
technological advancements, 8
Temple Mound Builders, 62
tepees, 48, 50
Thomas, Cyrus, 57
Tillamook, 33
Tlingit, 33–34, 81–82, 85
totem poles, 34
trade, 12, 15, 33, 44, 47, 49, 52–53, 60, 68
Trail of Tears, 89–90
tribal excavations, 9
tribes
  of Great Basin, 32, 36–37, 39
  of Great Plains, 6, 7, 23, 32, 44–53, 82, 84
  of Northeast, 54, 60, 65, 82
  of Northwest Coast, 32–33, 36, 82
  of Southeast, 54–55, 59, 84
  of Southwest, 9, 32, 40–41, 49
  warfare among, 78–85
  See also specific tribes
tuberculosis, 87
Tuskegee, 55
typhus, 87

U
U.S. Army, 91–92
Ute, 49

V
Van Buren, Martin, 89
villages
  Algonquian, 68–69
  fortifications for, 82, 84
  of Haudenosaunee, 69–72, 82
  of Mound Builders, 55–57, 59–60
  of Plains Woodland Native Americans, 47–48
  raids on, 85
  of Southeast, 55
  totem poles in, 34
visions, 43, 52, 68

W
Walapai, 41
Waldman, Carl
  on Native American religions, 43
  on pueblos, 41
  on tribelets, 39
Wampanoags, 65, 67
wampum, 74
war
  battle tactics, 84–85
  honor in, 78
  reasons for, 78
  rituals, 84–85
  tactics, 84–85
  weapons used in, 80–82, 84
warriors, prestige for, 78
Washington, 10, 14, 16, 32–33, 36
Washoe, 36
wattle lodges, 26
weaponry
  atlatls, 23–24, 27, 46, 80, 84
  bow and arrow, 6, 46–47, 50, 80
  Clovis point, 22–24, 26, 28
  defensive, 81, 82, 84
  European, 8, 88
  Folsom, 26, 28
  offensive, 81–82
West, 32–33
Western groups
  of California, 32–33, 38–39, 80
  of Great Basin, 32, 36–37, 39
  of Northwest Coast, 32–33, 36, 82
  of Southwest, 9, 32, 40–41, 49
white settlers
  adoption of Indian armor by, 84
  conquest by, 8, 86
  diseases brought by, 8, 87
whooping cough, 87
Wichita, 47
Wigwams, 68
Willey, Gordon, 33
Wintun, 39
Wounded Knee massacre, 7, 89–90

Y
Yakama, 37
Yuki, 39
Yuma, 41

Picture Credits

Cover, p. 79 Print Collector/Hulton Archive/Getty Images; pp. 4–5, 51, 77 Marzolino/Shutterstock.com; p. 6 (top) Kate Connes/Shutterstock.com; p. 6 (bottom) William Donahue/Thinkstock; p. 7 (top left) Nick Harris/Virgil Pomfret Agency/Thinkstock; pp. 7 (top right), 74 MPI/Stringer/Archive Photos/Getty Images; p. 7 (bottom left) Everett Historical/Shutterstock.com; p. 7 (bottom right) The Washington Post/Contributor/The Washington Post/Getty Images; p. 11 Homebrew Films Company/Getty Images; pp. 13, 38, 66, 67, 83 Courtesy of the Library of Congress; p. 14 Jon Greim/LOOP IMAGES/Getty Images; pp. 17, 55 Universal History Archive/Contributor/Universal Images Group/Getty Images; p. 19 Courtesy of the National Park Service; p. 24 Brian_Brockman/iStock/Thinkstock; pp. 26, 68 Nativestock.com/Marilyn Angel Wynn/Nativestock.com/Getty Images; p. 27 Carl & Ann Purcell/Getty Images; p. 28 Kurt Miller/Stocktrek Images/Getty Images; p. 31 GoodMood Photo/Shutterstock.com; p. 33 Kean Collection/Staff/Archive Photos/Getty Images; p. 34 rabbit75_ist/iStock/Thinkstock; p. 35 BMacZeroBot/Wikimedia Commons; pp. 36, 58 Richard A. Cooke/Getty Images; pp. 37, 45 Fototeca Storica Nazionale./Contributor/Hulton Archive/Getty Images; p. 40 John Cancalosi/Getty Images; pp. 41, 61 Pyty/Shutterstock.com p. 42 Scott T. Smith/Getty Images; p. 46 Barney Burstein/Corbis Historical/Getty Images; p. 48 Smallchief/Wikimedia Commons; p. 50 Photos.com/ Thinkstock; p. 63 Denise Panyik-Dale/Getty Images; p. 64 Franke Keating/Getty Images; p. 69 Stock Montage/Contributor/Archive Photos/Getty Images; p. 70 Peter Flass/Wikimedia Commons; p. 73 yui/Shutterstock.com; p. 81 John C. Hooten/Shutterstock.com; p. 87 Marilyn Angel Wynn/Nativestock/Getty Images; p. 89 Bettmann/Contributor/Bettmann/Getty Images; p. 91 Leonard Zhukovsky/Shutterstock.com.

About the Author

A prolific writer and former reading specialist, **Barbara M. Linde** has written more than 85 nonfiction books for children and young adults. She enjoys doing hands-on research and talking with experts for her books. Some of her titles include: *Rocket Scientists, Becoming a Supreme Court Justice, Native Peoples of California, Native Peoples of the Northeast, Native Peoples of the Southeast*, and *Heroes of the U.S. Army*. She lives with her husband, Jeffrey, and a large personal library, in Virginia.